Sophie & Juliet

Rags to Royalty

by

Carol Jeanne Kennedy

Publication Rights

Cover: *Portrait of Emperor Paul I's Daughters,* 1796, by Marie Louise Elisabeth Vigée-Lebrun (French, 1755-1842.) Public domain.

Dedications

To all my wonderful friends and family who helped me along the way in writing my novels. This book is dedicated to Don Knight, Billy Miller, Jean Gess, Carol Silvis, and Mary Burdick. Also, special thanks to Hennie Bekker whose musical compositions *Algonquin Trails* and *Stormy Sunday* provided the creative spark for *Winthrope*, followed by the rest of my Victorian Collection.

Other Great Novels by this Author

Winthrope – *Tragedy to Triumph*
The Arrangement – *Love Prevails*
Bobbin's Journal – *Waif to Wealth*
Poppy – *The Stolen Family*
Sophie & Juliet – *Rags to Royalty*
The Spinster – *Worth the Wait*
Holybourne – *The Magic of a Child*
A Novel Victorian Cookbook – *Forgotten Gems*

Links and Reviews

Visit the author's website: KennedyLiterary.com
Like on Facebook: caroljeannekennedy
Follow on Twitter @carol823599

Table of Contents

PROLOGUE

The "Mad King who lost America" (in English children's history books) King George III, had what was formerly thought to be a genetic disease, porphyria. More recently, scientists theorise that he had a mental illness, perhaps bipolar which came on in episodes of 'incessant loquacity,' but with rest and seclusion, he recovered from these bouts and continued to rule for 60 successful years, a dedicated and diligent king. His Majesty was a very conscientious ruler who believed in personal rule, albeit through constitutional means. He could speak to the ordinary man with humour, and he was afforded respect; he was very popular. But from 1788 he suffered from "some sort of debilitating disease," and by 1811 his health had deteriorated significantly. He subsequently became so deranged that his son George was made Prince Regent until King George III died in 1820. His beloved wife Charlotte died in 1818.

I have created this fictional romance novel not to make light of his mental illness nor to humiliate His Majesty, King George III, or his wife, Queen Charlotte, but only to bring a somewhat whimsical side to a real-life historical couple. For royalty in those days, with their privileged lifestyle, command over people, and with their ability to shape the world at whim, was a power unequalled in society. When they chose to, they could grant favours to the lesser rank, or by mere association, could esteem someone into high society and wealth. It was all too tempting to enjoy myself over this purely fictional tale. They were obviously a loving husband and wife, for they were married fifty-seven years and had fifteen children.

Chapter 1 – Lord Grayton Buries his Father

The Earl of Grayton buried his father with absolute relish. The tyrannical old boy was finally, absolutely, this time, really dead. His lordship remained at the grave site long after everyone had gone, watching the gravediggers heave shovelful after shovelful atop his father's coffin. Sniffing the air, he tossed a handful of dirt onto the mound and watched as the sexton tamped the moist black soil until it would sink no more.

"Well done, well done," said his lordship as he turned and walked into the foggy morning air. "And to think I thought this day would never come."

* * *

His busy London life and everything to do with a proper burial for his father had kept his lordship from his beloved boyhood country estate, Rosewood Park and his long-anticipated new life. Indeed, a new life now devoid of his father's rule, the stuffy formalities of the upper crust, the boring idleness of Court. All his life there was a gnawing restlessness to remake his dull existence and now, finally, resting in his own hands was his destiny to shape as he saw fit.

One of his first duties in his new life was to reacquaint himself with all the tenant farmers who had, up until now, been ignored, ill-used and overtaxed. Sitting upon his favourite leisure horse, Quill, he stared out over the valley below with his hound, Holly, obediently at his side.

"Fascinating intrigue, I must say, ol' girl. Indeed, if I am going to assume control of my life I must engage farmer Whitmore." He smiled. "And more importantly, I must first engage his wife, Anne."

* * *

It was a cool, rainy October day in the small village of Alton, located fifty or so rutty miles southwest of London and two miles from Lord Grayton's Rosewood Park. Between downpours, Anne Whitmore hurried from her small cottage to fetch a bucket of water. Hearing horses approach, she turned to see four quite spectacular dapple-greys pulling a closed carriage. "Dear me, it's Lord Grayton and his hound. I wonder why he comes?" She hurried back to the cottage, her bright red hair frizzed about her rain splattered translucent, freckled white face.

A streak of brilliant silver lightning pierced the thunderous path of black clouds as Sarah, her newborn, fussed. William, her husband, was busy stacking wood. Grayton's handsome equipage squeaked to a lumbering stop.

Anne stood at the threshold and curtsied as Grayton stepped from his carriage. "My lord, please come in and sit by our fire." She set the bucket down, wiped her rough red hands on her apron, and for being a little out of breath, apologised, "Excuse me, your lordship, would you like a mug of water?"

"No, Mrs Whitmore." He entered the cottage and glanced around, sniffing the air.

William entered, and being very tall, ducked to avoid the low opening. Finding Grayton, he gaped. "My lord, sir, you are very welcome."

Taking a chair at their rough-hewn sup table, the Earl looked about the cottage. "Ah, your fire is warm." He slipped lower in the chair, making himself very much at home. It smelled of fresh apples and green pasture grass. Through one wavy-glassed window, a stream of gold pierced the dark cottage air. He watched the unsettled gold dust glittering in the sun's beam as it touched quietly upon the white-washed wooden floor. There were but two chairs in the kitchen, and a barrel. On a shelf sat wooden bowls, pewterware, and spoons. A few lit candles flickered mild shades of yellow into the dank, heavy air.

"Yes, I like it here very much."

Anne curtsied. "Thank you, sir. I'm glad you find it pleasing." Just then Sarah began to wail. "Oh, beg pardon, your lordship," said Anne.

Grayton stood. "Bring your child to me. I must see it, Mrs Whitmore." He drew off his spotless kidskin gloves and tossed them onto the table.

Anne exchanged glances with her husband. "But of course, my lord." She hurried to Sarah, wrapped her in her nicest blanket, and brought her to him.

" 'Two births, Grayton.' His Majesty spoke those words a few months ago to me." He turned to Anne. "You mentioned the good omen when we first met."

Sarah stopped fussing at his voice.

William stood silent, confusion plain as day on his face.

"Indeed I did, your lordship," said Anne as she glanced at her child in amazement, for she was now cooing. "I remember our conversation exactly, my lord. My husband told me of the two shooting stars crossing paths in the night sky just as I gave birth to Sarah."

William nodded. "Indeed, my lord." He opened the door and stood on the threshold. "I stood right here and witnessed the most excellent of omens—two shooting stars crossed paths in the heavens just as Sarah was born."

Grayton nodded. "Well, standing on the balcony at Norfolk-House, London, at King George's birthday ball, I witnessed the very same precisely when my son, Henry, was born."

"Our families are blessed it seems," said Anne. A gracious smile spread across her face.

"Whitmore, are you going to stand there forever holding that wood?" said Grayton with half a smile.

"Oh, no, my lord, ah, indeed, not." He tossed the logs into the woodbin and brushed the dirt from his hands, nodding respectfully. "Thank you, my lord. They were a trifle heavy."

"I thought so. Well, as I was about to say, there is more to the story of our children being born at exactly the same time two shooting stars arced. Indeed, when His Majesty learned of the prophetic sight in the Heavens, he raised his ornate silver cup and from his lips declared, 'there were two births, Grayton. You must go and find your son's mate.' "

Anne lifted Sarah, who was now cooing at his lordship. Her expressions were giggly and sweet, pink and shiny.

Looking amused, the Earl gazed down at her sweet, animated face. "Sarah?" Her tiny hands flailed about, apparently mesmerised by his shiny brass buttons, by the showy feathers in his hat, his black beard, and his deep, resonant voice. "Ah, yes, you are the very one."

Anne and William laughed as their daughter clearly stole his lordship's heart.

"I am now convinced that your daughter is the second birth His Majesty spoke about."

Anne and William stood in silent awe.

"Indeed, therefore, I will share with you my plan." He

glanced from Anne to William. "You shall school my son in morals and manners."

The Whitmores stood quiet and confused, daring not to say one word; very much unaware of what was next to come.

"I must not have a nanny who is cold and indifferent as Mrs Brown, his present nursemaid. Heaven knows she never smiles." He shook his head. "She is too strict and forbidding. Haha," he picked up his gloves and slapped them on his knee, "I dare say she does not care two straws for me, and absolutely detests when I take Henry on jaunts. Lady Grayton becomes overly excited because of her. Yes, I have no doubt Mrs Brown will leave her mark on my four daughters. I am afraid they will all become quite ruined." He stood. "But she shall not mark my son as my father marked me."

"But your lordship, what are we to do for your son?" said Anne.

Just then there came a scratch at the door. When William opened it, a black whirl bounded past him. Prancing in with great delight, his lordship's beloved hound, Holly, wiggled to his side.

"Oh, dear me," Grayton laughed, "this mad, foolish, madrigal hound, has once again found me." He glanced at Anne. "Do forgive the beast, madam. She's my very shadow."

William and Anne laughed politely.

"Oh, sir, she is no bother," said William, "no bother at all."

"I don't believe it, William." His lordship settled the dog at his side with a stern, "Sit. Ah, where were we then? Oh, yes, Henry. Well, school him as you would your own daughter, Sarah."

The Whitmores exchanged glances, clearly stunned.

"I mean to leave my son with you all day, every day. I will have him brought to you in the morning, and I will have someone bring him home in the evening. Oh, not to worry, I shall reward you handsomely. I know you both are the very ones to plant good seeds into my only son."

"But, your lordship, what of Lady Grayton? Would she not be offended by common people tutoring your son?" asked Anne.

"Her ladyship has not a word to say upon the matter. She has four ruined daughters to her credit, and I will not have a spoiled, ruinous, ne'er-do-well, for a son."

With tears in her eyes, Anne gently laid Sarah on the table and removed her little wrap. "Sir, I wish it of you to first witness her imperfect form. Perhaps you may ..."

His lordship glanced down at the infant's deformed leg, being a few inches shorter than the other. "Pity, pity." Turning, he tugged at his gloves as he kept staring down at her. "You must treat Henry as you do Sarah, in all ways and manner." He approached the door, opened it and stopped. "I shall bring him to you in the morning. You must not address him titled, reserve that only in public."

Anne snuggled Sarah to her breast. "Oh, indeed, sir."

Anne and William had no choice but to honour Grayton's strange request.

Standing at the open door, his lordship smiled at Anne. "Mrs Whitmore, I found the Holybourne Orphanage."

"Oh, indeed, my lord, my sister Jane wrote me of your visit expressing how kind your spirit."

"How kind my spirit?" He twisted the tip of his thick black moustache. "Indeed."

"Her words exactly, my lord."

He smiled, adjusted his hat, and left.

As they stood watching his carriage amble away, William turned to his wife. "The orphanage, Anne? Why would his lordship visit the orphanage?"

"Last month at our faire, his lordship inquired of me about the silver-haired maiden who had charge of so many beggarly children running about. I explained that she was my sister, Jane, and that we were both raised in the orphanage. She alone remained when the other teachers left for better prospects."

William nodded. "Indeed, despite her circumstances, Jane is a comely beauty."

* * *

Grayton was truthful when he said he would pay them handsomely. Soon after his proposal, he bestowed upon the Whitmores many cows, oxen, foodstuffs, furniture, horses, even a chaise and carriage.

William added another room to the cottage. His lordship rewarded them financially, as well. So much so, that William didn't tend the fields any longer. He had not the time, but to keep up with Grayton's gifts, he had to keep building and improving his cottage.

Helen Whitmore, William's mother, sat in her son's cottage overwhelmed at his good fortune. Helping Anne fold Henry's clothes, she sighed, "All these fine things we have sewn for Henry and they are always returned, never worn."

"For my life, Mother, I cannot imagine having so many things to wear that the child cannot be clothed with the same thing more than once." Anne shook her head.

"Such wealth is beyond me."

"Aye, Mother, I agree, but we shall never know that now, will we?"

"I don't imagine so, Anne, but the way Lord Grayton sends things to your step, I should wonder, for soon your cottage will make two of mine."

"Indeed, Mother, he is far more generous than his miserly father who only came to complain."

* * *

Henry was brought to the Whitmores' every day as promised. There was never a day or a holiday missed. At each visit, Henry would first run to see Sarah, for they had become inseparable. When Grayton would personally bring Henry, he would affectionately bid his father farewell, as he was taught. Sarah would limp to his lordship and pout if he did not kiss her as well—the bond was set.

Chapter 2 – A Surprise Party

When Lord Grayton and his son, Henry, left Rosewood Park's pebbly roadway onto the Winchester Road to Alton, the rain suddenly turned to a gentle mist, the air now a fine spray. It was such a morning that lent itself to reflection. Henry, propped up on his pillow, wiped the carriage's fogged window with his gloved hand, silent as the glass he stared through. Ten years had passed since Grayton embarked on setting his son to become a good and honest man under the tutelage of the Whitmores and he was satisfied with the outcome.

Grayton watched his son with a growing sense of pleasure. Indeed, he seemed more than pleased by Henry's developed good nature and fine manners, and he was always proud to hear how well he was doing in his lessons. Moreover, he was so impressed by his son's most excellent progress that an intriguing thought entered his mind—*I shall plan a surprise for Henry's tenth birthday; and where else could it be celebrated than our ancestral home in the great gardens of Rosewood Park. Everyone in the village shall be invited.* He patted Henry on the head congratulating himself on such a splendid idea. *Oh, indeed, and we mustn't forget the little orphans from Holybourne. Capital, capital.*

Henry noticed his father's excitement. "What is it, Papa? Do you have something to say?"

Grayton cleared his throat, looking smug. "You shall soon see, Henry, you shall soon see."

Arriving at the Whitmores', Grayton now found himself in a very happy mood. "Mrs Whitmore, I have thought of a wonderful idea to celebrate Henry and Sarah's tenth birthdays."

Anne stood, obediently listening, as usual. "Indeed, my lord, I must hear it."

"I will have a grand garden party at Rosewood Park. Everyone in the village is welcome. I would ask that you extend the invitation to me. Oh, and one must not forget your sister, Miss Stewart, she may bring the orphans."

Anne gushed at such a prospect. "Oh, Lord Grayton, I find that a very kind thing for you and your family to do. Why, June is but two months away. Henry talks of his mother and sisters so often, and since we have not met your family, we shall indeed look forward to coming. Oh, and to bring the orphans to such an event will bring much happiness to their hearts, they have so little, sir."

Well pleased with himself, Grayton smiled with a nod. "Indeed so, Mrs Whitmore, I thought as much."

His lordship had not mentioned his grand plan to his wife since the idea had come upon him so suddenly, but he would inform her when he returned to Rosewood Park that very day. For a few minutes at least, he was happy at the thought, but then his mood turned to melancholy. *How am I to present such an idea to Elizabeth? A garden party for Henry and Sarah? Dear me.*

Lady Elizabeth was not one for festive balls and idle pleasures for the children—for any children. Such favours made her quite nervous and cross. *But there is time enough to inform her of my plans,* he felt relieved, *for June is a full two months away.*

* * *

Lord Grayton had put off informing his wife of Henry's garden party for several weeks now and questioned himself about his hesitancy. He felt silly over the entire affair and decided to inform her of his plans this morning, over breakfast. He thought for a second longer and then wisely corrected himself. "*After* breakfast, for I am famished."

Somehow the reaction from his wife did not surprise him. The news mortified her and their four daughters: Margaret, Mary, Victoria and Elizabeth. They were embarrassed that such a gathering would be in *their* garden.

"What should the neighbours think upon the occasion," cried his wife.

The earl stood firm. "You *will* all attend the party, Elizabeth." He glanced at each of his daughters and then to his wife. "Henry has grown into an unspoiled young man. Why, he has a kind heart and purpose. We fish together, throw stones together, and soon he and I shall ride together. Perhaps you have conveniently failed to remember how His Majesty carried on so about me finding Henry's mate ... the twin birth? The crossing of stars? You know very well, Elizabeth, for it has been well understood for a very long time now that Sarah Whitmore is that very child—

Henry's mate."

In a huff, Lady Elizabeth tossed her napkin to the table. "Please, my lord, spare me."

"We shall celebrate both children's births." He gulped the last of his tea feeling very satisfied that he dealt his snooty family a proper set-down. After all, it was his destiny to become a good and thoughtful human being, never forgetting his tyrannical father for an instant.

Lady Elizabeth and her daughters glared at him in disbelief. No one uttered a sound.

His daughter Margaret, the most spoiled, stood. "Papa, may I be excused?"

He studied her plate, the food suitably consumed. "Very well, you may."

Rising from the table, she turned her nose in the air and proceeded toward the door. She was the eldest at sixteen and most pompous in disposition. Just before she quitted the dining room, she made a parting comment to her mother, "Really, Mama, must I be witness to such a scene with Henry's *heathen friends* in our garden?"

Her sisters, Mary, Victoria, and Elizabeth made faces, nodding in total agreement.

Lady Elizabeth glared at her husband. "My lord, pray tell, how should we entertain an entire village of ignorant, filthy farmers with their broken and shabby wagons? The ruts they shall make in the roads; their oxen and horses will crowd the flowers. Oh, the smell. Think of the smell, John. Oh, it shall not be tolerated. What have we done to deserve this?"

He sat back smiling at the snobs. "What have you done? What *haven't* you done?"

Her ladyship stood. "Excuse me, sir, I am going to spit up."

Mary and Victoria followed her from the room. Elizabeth, ten and two years of age, remained.

Grayton watched his wife and daughters leave. He turned to Elizabeth, who was two years older than Henry and not one to hold her tongue. "Well, Lizzy, why are you still here? I thought surely you would follow your mother and sisters."

She frowned. "Papa, you will celebrate Henry's birthday in grand fashion, but you forgot mine just a fortnight past."

He frowned. "Is that so?"

She looked him straight in the eye. "That is so, Papa, and sir, why do you not come to see *us* like you always do Henry?"

He studied her deep-set blue eyes, her wrinkled freckled little nose. "*Us?* Are you speaking for your sisters?"

She set her fork down. "No, they do not care two straws for you, Papa."

His brows arched at her frankness. "And what about you, Lizzy? Do you care two straws for your Papa?"

She squirmed, wiped her brow, directing her eyes downcast. "Well maybe, but I don't know you as a father, Papa. You are a father to Henry, but not me." Her dark blue eyes sparkled like chips of ice.

"Is that so?"

"Yes, Papa, that is so."

"How old are you, Lizzy?"

"I am ten and two, sir." She sat up straight, still studying his every move.

Grayton glanced out the window. It was a sunny day, and he had decided earlier that he would ride to the Whitmores' rather than bother with the carriage.

"Lizzy, I wish to ride this morning. Would you like to join me?"

She scooted her chair back and stood. With a wide smile, she nodded. "Oh, indeed, Papa." Her face sobered as she plopped back down in her chair. "But I have French lessons this morning." She folded her arms and sighed heavily. "And we are to entertain Lady Hammish after lunch, I cannot go."

"Well, I do believe I can arrange to have your French lessons postponed for another day, and I think your mother and sisters are quite capable of entertaining Lady Hammish without your help."

Her head bobbed in absolute delight. She detested Lady Hammish and her stupid, nippy, nasty little pug. Hurrying to her father's side, she took up his hand, startling him.

He tweaked her nose. "Well, well, let us be on with it then." With an air of triumph, they left the room together. Stopping at Mrs Brown's classroom, his lordship informed her that Lizzy's French lessons would be postponed until tomorrow. "And inform Lady Grayton that Lady Elizabeth has gone riding with her father."

Behind their back, the grumpy old Mrs Brown dumped Lizzy's lessons into the trash bin. Wiping her hands in disgust, she mumbled, "Humph, do this, do that ..."

Grayton and Lizzy walked to the mews holding hands, silent as they traversed the crunchy, well-worn gravel footpath.

He glanced down at his daughter. "Lizzy, tell me, do you get on well with the governess?"

Her little nose wrinkled, her brow furrowed deeply. "No, Papa, I hate Mrs Brown." She took her hand from his. "Look, Papa," she held up her knuckles for him to examine them in detail. "As you can clearly see, sir, they are red and bruised from her pointing stick always hitting them. I cannot learn French as well as Mary, Margaret and Victoria. I hate being laughed at. I am always last it seems."

"Well, perhaps we can change all that."

"Really, Papa?"

He looked at her frilly-laced morning dress. "Daughter, are you going to ride in that frock?"

"Oh, Papa, I, I didn't think you were of a serious mind and that you really wanted me to ride with you."

Grave as any judge, he nodded. "Oh, but I do. I do."

She lit up with a smile, the sweetest sort of smile. "Oh, sir, it shall not take me long to change."

He laughed as she bolted from his side, kicked off her shoes, and ran quite wild through two petticoats. Nearing the stewards' entry, she tossed off her bonnet and yelped. The gardeners laughed as she whooshed by.

Grayton looked up and witnessed Mrs Brown's expression of horror at the sight of Elizabeth's most unladylike conduct. With a smirk, he removed his hat and bowed to her. With an indignant turn, she quickly left the window as Margaret, Mary and Victoria followed.

Chapter 3 – Henry's Garden Party

It turned out to be a lovely June morning for Henry and Sarah's garden birthday party. *It is an omen that such a wonderful day shall end so.* With that happy thought settling him, Grayton turned from the window and addressed his wife, "My dear lady, I would wish it of you to dress down this day. Being polite to our less fortunate *guests* would be thoughtful, indeed."

She pursed her lips. "Sir, ever since your father died, your odd-mannered demands have become quite impossible. Dress down? Whatever do you mean, sir, dress down? After all, they are just farmers, certainly nothing to take notice of. Indeed, I shall *not* dress down. I shall not, nor shall my daughters."

His lordship sighed. But, he knew better than to reason with her. "Well then, Elizabeth, you may dress as you please, but with restraint, with restraint. I wish that of you, wife."

She frowned. "Restraint? I should wonder at using restraint. I would wish you would do the same, my lord. These past months you have become exceedingly odd in your demands. I am vexed that you should grovel in the mud with those farmers. Oh, spare me the torment and ridicule from my friends over your silly, stupid whim to entertain a ten-year-old boy and his so-called *mate*, Sarah." She snorted, "Foolish business to be sure."

"Madam, that is quite enough."

"Your son is but a child and not yet capable of reasoning, nor for that matter, choosing his own proper society. You should be ashamed."

"Very well, Elizabeth, you do not need to join our party, but I insist my daughters are to be present, and sensibly dressed." He left, closing the door firmly behind him.

Lady Elizabeth felt relieved at being released from the *lawn affair*. Finally, she had prevailed upon her husband. Standing at her long mirror, she tied her bonnet under her left ear and huffed, "The silly fool."

She planned to leave the Great House as soon as may be. Her daughters were to fend for themselves. After all, they had the most excellent guidance of Mrs Brown, who was to attend the affair in her stead. As for Henry, she shook her head. "I fear he shall be like his father in all ways and will find nothing to mortify his little bones over the entire squalid matter. Let him become the object of ridicule, what shall I care over the calamity. I have done my duty in lending objection, and now being quite put out of the absurdity, I shall leave quietly, before the disgusting hordes arrive."

Her ladyship stepped merrily down the stairs thinking of her visit with her sister, Lady Catherine, in London. A fifty-mile journey was a lengthy one, and she planned on returning the following day. She had already been stewing a goodly amount of time, forming the *garden party debacle* into neat little boxes that she may present each to her sister. *Surely she will swoon at the news.*

* * *

From his room, Henry watched his mother board the carriage. He wondered why she never kissed him goodbye like Anne and Sarah always did. He shook his head. "But Mama never kisses me." As he wiped his eyes, he suddenly spotted oxen on the distant hill pulling carts.

"They are come!" He shouted, jumping up and down. "They are come to my party!" He was so excited that he scrambled out his window and hastily climbed down the wild rose vine trellis. No matter that a thorn ripped his trousers. His dog, Willie, spotted him and the two scurried to the hill that was filling fast with his *other family* from Alton. Spotting the Holybourne orphans, he ran and jumped with them all ... proudly dressed in their cleanest rags, shoeless.

He soon found William. "Sir, you did not use the road there?" He pointed.

"Aye, Master Henry didn't want to rut the road."

"William, you must not call me Master ..."

"Oh, but indeed I must. For now we are in public. I know my place, young man."

Henry shrugged. "Very well, William, I suppose you are right." He noticed his mother's carriage move away. "There goes my mother, sir. She is going to London. She finds no happiness in your visit here." Henry waved goodbye to her, but she stuck her nose in the air and turned away.

Henry smiled up at William, ignoring his mother's snub. "I am glad you are here, and so is my father." In his next breath, he cried, "May I ride your ox, sir? I shall hold tight. Oh, please, sir."

William laughed as he lifted Henry onto the huge, gentle ox.

Suddenly Lizzy appeared at his side out of breath and panting. Her thick black hair stuffed up high into her yellow bonnet, sweat beaded on her upper lip. "Oh, please, William, may I lead the ox?"

He handed her the rope. "Indeed, Lady Elizabeth, you may."

Henry squinted in the sun's glare. "But do not go so very fast, Lizzy."

She rolled her eyes. "I know very well how to lead an ox, Henry." With a sigh and shake of her head, she led them away.

* * *

As Lord Grayton stood before the many tents and tables in the garden, he caught sight of his son riding the ox, Lizzy leading the way. He shook his head in awe. *I never would have thought she would do such a thing.* He felt a tug on his sleeve.

"Papa," Margaret pointed, "Henry is riding that beast. Dear God, he shall fall and become impaled on those ghastly horns. And, mind Lizzy, sir, she is leading the ghastly parade. You must stop this immediately."

The Earl put his arm around her shoulder. "Daughter, calm yourself. Can't you see the smile on your brother's face? The happiness in his manner? Why, he is wild with delight. I dare say if he runs himself through, he shall die a happy boy."

Her jaw dropped.

Her sister, Mary, stood behind her and overheard the entire conversation. She bid her tongue a respite, lest her father throw her into the ox's path. Then, from the corner of her eye, she caught an odd movement and tugged on Margaret's arm. "Look there at that little girl." She pointed.

Margaret eyed Sarah. "One leg is very much shorter than the other," she whispered.

Mary stared. "Oh, I have never seen a freak before." She watched in horror as Sarah limped past.

But Margaret was not in the least bit appalled at such a disfigurement. She was always fascinated with ways in which she could splinter a wounded animal; help a bird that broke its wing; the imperfect body fascinated her. She would steal away at night into the library and read books on anatomy, human or animal.

Sarah, being quite aware of people staring, limped away. She found that if she simply smiled at them, they would move on. Being taught to respect her betters, she curtsied, but her good foot became stuck in cow dung, and she fell.

Mary guffawed at such a sight.

Within an instant, Henry slid from the ox and ran to her side. "There now, Sarah," he steadied her. Taking his handkerchief from his pocket, he wiped her hands and frock.

Margaret and Mary watched in bewilderment as Henry brushed the dung from her frock.

Mary's nose wrinkled. "He is touching the little freak's hand. Oh, how disgusting. Her name is Sarah? Surely that is not *the* Sarah Whitmore from Alton—Henry's so-called mate?" She covered her mouth in horror. "Oh, that mother shall faint straight away."

Chapter 4 – Shocking News Comes to Rosewood Park

The next morning after the garden party, Margaret stood in disbelief at the news. Lord Grayton sunk into his chair, dumbfounded. Mary wept as Victoria stared blankly at the floor. Lizzy sat at her father's feet. Henry had just returned from the Whitmores' when the shocking news came to Rosewood Park.

"How did it happen, Byron?" Grayton dropped his head into his hands in anguish at the news of his wife's death.

"Well, my lord," said the magistrate, "Lady Grayton and her sister Lady Catherine were riding in the chaise when suddenly an out-of-control carriage raced them by, startling their team. Lady Catherine's horse bolted and pulled the chaise wildly down the road crashing into a tree. Lady Catherine suffered a few cuts, and that is all we know at this moment—I am truly sorry, your lordship." With that, the humble magistrate bowed and made way a little distance from the grieving family. "My lord, is there anything more I may do?"

Grayton shook his head. "No, leave us now, leave us to our grief." Excusing him with a flick of his wrist, his lordship crumpled back into his chair, devastated. He felt guilty for having a cross word with his wife just before she left.

"But, Papa, how should this happen to our family, we are wealthy," cried Victoria.

"Death plays no favourites," he said in a terse whisper.

Margaret glared at Henry. "First off, Mother should not have been there."

Henry lifted his eyes to her, crying as well, but he was too young to fully understand the implication. He was not too young, though, to catch the hatred in her voice. "Maggy, why are you angry at me?" His lower lip quivered.

Margaret wisely kept her hurtful words to herself; Henry was but an innocent child. However, her feelings toward her father would not be denied. "If it were not for your disgraceful garden party, Father, my beloved mother would still be here with us. I shall hate you, Father!" She ran from the room.

* * *

As the months passed, everything Margaret touched turned to tatters. She often spilt her wine at supper—breaking many fine glasses. Her needlework was no longer fine and deft, but crude and ugly. Her manner had become aggressive and bold. She was rude even to Victoria, her favourite; never mind Mary, Elizabeth and Henry—they were treated as if they were invisible.

Lord Grayton continued to take Henry to the Whitmores,' and now Mary hinted about going along. She wanted away from the cruel and spiteful Margaret. Adding to the flames, Lizzy spoke often about her happy visits with Henry while in Alton.

"Well, I dare say they must live too common for my taste," said Victoria. With a sneer, she added, "After all, they are mere cottagers."

Mary, eager to join Lizzy, disagreed, "Oh, not so common, I would imagine."

Victoria was beginning to feel left out. Margaret no longer wished her company. And now, to think, Mary was cosy with Lizzy, and the two were to angle away their days away at the Whitmores.' Whatever was she to do? Besides that, Mrs Brown and Margaret were becoming very secretive and guarded these many months.

"Lizzy," said Victoria in tempered desperation, "I would not mind in the least to go visiting with you and Mary to the Whitmores." Her brows knitted. "It has become too droll here anymore."

"Oh, I think not, Victoria," replied Lizzy with a shrug." Now feeling very much in control—having her older sister beg for *her* company. "Indeed, there would be no room, what with our plans and all."

"Plans?"

"Indeed, Mrs Whitmore's mother, Granny Whitmore, wishes to teach me French. Oh, oui, and probably sew me many nice things. I really do not think there is room enough in their *very* small cottage. Anyway, you have often said that they must not live in comfort."

Victoria's mouth twitched. "I do not remember ever saying anything of the sort, Lizzy."

"Because you are stupid, that is why."

Victoria gasped, tears flooded her eyes.

Lizzy covered her mouth in shame. Putting her arm around Victoria's shoulder, she apologised, "Oh, Vicky, I am sorry. That was mean of me to say such a thing. Truly I am sorry. I am sure Papa will want us *all* to go the Whitmores, except Maggy, of course."

Victoria's mood lightened as she dabbed her eyes. "Oh, of course not, but she wouldn't come anyway."

"Oh, for sure."

They once more they began their sisterly chatter, excitedly making plans to visit Alton when Margaret suddenly entered the room with Mrs Brown—a dark cloud hovered over the two.

The sisters huddled closer to the fire, ignoring them.

Mrs Brown hemmed, "Young ladies, I have news for you. Your father and I have discussed the idea of you all going to London to visit your Aunt Catherine. I must say it will be a lighter venue than Rosewood Park. Indeed, away for several months in London will do you all good."

Margaret looked down her nose at the girls. "Oh, I quite agree, Mrs Brown, such a delightful idea, indeed." She knew she had lost all power over her sisters. They no longer cared if, or when, she spoke. She could feel their cool indifference at every turn, and felt envious of their secretive little chats, hand gestures, and plans.

Lizzy frowned. "Mrs Brown, just *when* are we to visit Aunt Catherine?"

Margaret smirked. "Soon, I dare say, for I am exceedingly unhappy here anymore. A change in atmosphere and society should do you all good, I am sure of it."

"Not for a month, I should wonder," said Lizzy, "for we are to visit the Whitmores' very often with father now that the weather has mellowed."

Mary set down her stitchery. "Yes, and Victoria and I are to go along."

Ignoring her sister, Margaret smiled. "Father is in agreement with the visit. He thinks it a very good plan that you are all exposed more to London society. He feels you are becoming too wayward here. Indeed, you must not be absent during the Season and be under Aunt Catherine's proper influence and guidance."

"We will leave Monday next."   With that Mrs Brown left the room.

Margaret stayed to witness the disappointment on their faces. "You are all traitors, the three of you. Mother would certainly not be proud of her little darlings now." She glared.

Mary and Victoria kept their heads low, fiddling with their sewing, whispering, tittering. Lizzy took up a book.

"Lizzy," said Margaret with a smirk, "as of late I have noticed you are reading very many books."

"Oh, indeed, I am studying French, Maggy," she said, without taking her eyes from the book.

Margaret hated the nickname *Maggy*. But, not wanting to show her irritation, she smiled. "But why, dear sister, when you have not yet even begun to master proper English?"

Victoria burst out laughing. In haste, though, she covered her mouth.

"For your information, Maggy, I am studying French because Papa will be taking me to Paris."

Mary and Victoria's mouth gaped. Never before had Lizzy ever lied (that they knew of).

"Well, we will see about that," said Margaret. She left the room in a huff, slamming the door behind her.

"Oh, you mustn't have lied to her, Lizzy. She will tell Mrs Brown for sure," said Mary in a great snit.

Victoria tweaked Lizzy's nose. "Indeed, Papa will be furious with you. Hurry to Margaret and take back the lie. Hurry before she tells Mrs Brown."

Lizzy crossed her arms in defiance. "Of course I shall not. Besides, Papa does not care two straws what Mrs Brown thinks, and if I should see him first, I shall tell him of *our* plan."

"Our plan? What do you mean, Lizzy?" said Victoria.

"I mean, I shall tell Papa we do not want to go see grieving Aunt Catherine in London, we would rather travel to Paris instead. If we three plead with him, he'll surely take us there. Oui?"

They heard the door close ever so softly. "Oh, no," said Mary, "someone has been snooping."

Lizzy ran to the door and opened it only to see the swish of Mrs Brown's flowing garb move down the hall. "Holy fish, it was Mrs Brown."

"Oh, dear me, we must reach Papa before she does." Mary stood with her hands on her hips, fretting. "Oh, but how shall we find him?"

"Well, simple that, he is of course at the Whitmores.' We shall go to him," said Lizzy flatly, "but, we must leave immediately."

Chapter 5 – The Village of Alton

The three sisters arrived in the quiet little village just a little past noon that very day. As Lizzy stepped from the carriage, she was greeted by only a few of the village children. Glancing around, she shook head. "How very strange, everyone has gone."

Mary and Victoria stepped down glancing about, sniffing the air, wrinkling their noses.

"So this is where Henry spends most of his days," said Mary in wonder.

A few village children stood in awe of the beautiful, elegant young ladies; never before had so many come to Alton all at once.

Victoria seemed particularly enthralled by all the attention. One little girl stared at her fine, white, red-spotted, muslin frock.

"May I touch one of the red dots, ma'am?"

"Certainly you may," Victoria giggled. "Come, you may touch all of them, if you wish."

Mary glanced around with a frown. "Where have all the people gone? I should think there would be many here about."

"They have all gone to yonder meadow with our master, Lord Grayton," one little girl pointed. "There is to be a new road built, but for the trees, it will take much work. Most everyone in the village is there. It is to be a great road, and everyone is happy over it."

Victoria frowned, dabbing her nose. "Happy over a mere road?"

"Oh, miss, the new road will take half the time to reach market," said another one of the children. "And it will have a great many stones piled onto it."

Lizzy gestured toward the meadow. "Oh, look there, Mrs Whitmore comes."

Anne was well along with child, her walk was awkward and slow. She soon spied the carriage and the Misses Graytons. With a huge smile, she opened her arms and welcomed them all. "Oh, what a grand surprise, I have been over yonder field," she gestured with her head, "where our new road is to be built."

Anne entered the cottage. "Come in." She removed her wrap and hung it on a wall peg. "Look there, a soft fire and broth in the pot." She hung her bonnet next to her wrap and waddled slowly toward the huge fire pit. "I shall add another log to the fire."

Anne invited everyone to sit at the rough-hewn sup table and enjoy a bowl of broth. She laboured about the huge kitchen hearth when an astounding thing happened.

"Please, Mrs Whitmore," said Mary as she stood, "we can certainly help ourselves. Tell us what to do. We should be helping *you*, please sit and rest."

Victoria nodded. "Indeed, I will break the bread. I know how to do that at least."

Lizzy remained silent, staring at Anne's swollen belly.

"Mary, bring the broth to the table," said Victoria.

Indeed, each little lady was busy worrying about their own stomachs, taking away their worry over Anne's.

Lizzy looked up from her bowl. "Mrs Whitmore, will our father be coming back soon?"

"Well, now, I am not at all certain."

Lizzy was nervous that by some stroke of bad luck, Mrs Brown should find her father before she did. So, the kindhearted Anne was told of their predicament. Indeed, the sisters could not hide their trepidation at being caught in a falsehood.

Victoria nodded. "Oh, that Lizzy told such a bold lie about going to Paris. If we do not soon speak with Papa, Mrs Brown's fury will consume our very souls. Indeed, Mrs Whitmore, we are in deep trouble, and only Papa can extricate us from her wrath."

Just then Henry and Sarah came in all a rush, laughing and giggling.

Henry stopped short, staring in disbelief. He found his sisters sitting at the table. "I don't believe such a sight. What brings you?"

Victoria watched Sarah limp to her mother's side. "Mrs Whitmore, do suppose your next child will be a freak like her?"

Mary and Lizzy gasped. The look on Mrs Whitmore's face was so crushing that to take back the words a thousand times could never erase the hurt.

Victoria knew instantly the terrible anguish she had inflicted on this dear, loving woman, and innocent child, Sarah. She covered her mouth in shame. "Oh, forgive me the words, ma'am. I am truly sorry."

Anne brought Sarah to her side and hugged her. Henry

glared at Victoria. The room grew silent as glass.

"Sarah," said her mother now recovered, "you know you were born special and walk differently than us. But, we do not use the word 'freak' because it is a word that describes another person in a hurtful manner. Lady Victoria said that word because she didn't know better. She did not mean to say such a hurtful word. She is too dear, that I am sure."

Victoria nodded. "Indeed, Sarah, forgive me the words."

Sarah limped to her. "Lady Victoria," she gently pulled her hands away from her shamed face, "I forgive you. Please, do not cry any more."

Just then there came a clamour from outside—another carriage had arrived. When Henry unlatched the door, there stood his sister, Margaret. Mary and Lizzy jumped up, stunned.

"How did she find us?" whispered Mary.

"Welcome, Lady Margaret," said Anne with a smile. "Well, this is a very special day, indeed. Now we have all the Misses Graytons here at once. I cannot believe my good fortune. Please, come in and take a chair, there by the hearth."

Margaret walked in and quickly perused the cottage. "Well, certainly not so dark or smallish after all. I am wrong, then, of my vision that it was ill-fit for Henry to spend time here."

Anne nodded. "I am glad you find it so, Lady Margaret." She noticed her searching eyes, the subtle twitch of her nose. "Ma'am, may I offer you a bit of broth and bread? You must be very hungry from such a ride."

"No, Mrs Whitmore, thank you," said Margaret. Suddenly catching sight of her sisters huddling together, her tone changed. "I am here only in search of my sisters, food being the last thing on my mind." She glared at Mary. "I found that I had, in haste, travelled to Chawton. I spent time searching for them there when I happened to mention to the footman where you live, Mrs Whitmore. My driver knew immediately of the possibility of their error, and brought me to Alton."

Lizzy lifted her chin. "Why have you come, Maggy? *We* have come to see Papa and ... Henry. We are, at present, waiting for Papa to return."

On the verge of tears, Margaret took in a great breath. The veins on her forehead protruded, as they usually did when she was severely provoked. "When you left without informing Mrs Brown, she became more than disgusted and resigned her position. Indeed, packed her things and left for London."

The sisters exchanged glances of glee.

"And so I have been riding for many hours searching for you. I was worried sick. You could have at least left a note." Glancing at Mrs Whitmore's *condition*, she calmed her voice. "I even thought you might be silly enough to venture to Paris."

A nervous laugh escaped Lizzy, "Ha, Paris, we shall not go to Paris for a fortnight. But, that, of course, is Papa's choice."

Margaret shook her head. "Does Papa know of the current turmoil and trouble there with the French Emperor, Comte de Grasse, Lizzy?"

Victoria and Mary shook their heads. "Grasse?"

Anne suddenly slumped into her chair, grabbing her stomach, groaning.

Margaret hurried to her side. "Mrs Whitmore, are you feeling ill?"

"My baby is coming ..." she moaned, "it's moving low. Please, bring my mother ... she is but next door."

Lizzy ran to the door. "I will fetch her." But in her excitement, she turned right instead of left, and when finding no one in any of the cottages, covered her eyes in despair. "Oh, fish! Where is everyone?" She envisioned Anne's stomach ripping open this very minute. "Oh, where is everyone?"

A little girl passing by overheard her. "They are in yonder meadow," she pointed. "Come I'll take you there."

* * *

Margaret hurriedly tossed her cashmere shawl, bonnet and gloves onto the table, and calmly gave orders to her sisters: "Victoria, boil water. Mary, search for clean rags." She had read enough about the human anatomy and medicine from her father's library to know a good bit about the birthing process. She gently brushed the hair away from Anne's perspiring face. "Ma'am, are you able to walk to your bed?"

"I, I think so." She slowly stood, holding her stomach. "I think I can make it that far, Lady Margaret." She doubled up and moaned. "But, please find my mother-in-law, her name is Helen Whitmore. Oh, my child is coming." She held her stomach. "Hurry."

Margaret slowly led her to bed. "Mary, spread the blankets for her to lie on. Tell Vicky to hurry with the water." She then quickly removed Anne's clothing.

"Lady Margaret, I am very surprised at your manner," said

Anne, trying to calm her breathing. "How well you know of these things. I am ..." She doubled up again. A clear, water-like fluid ran down her legs, pooling on the floor.

"Hurry, Vicky, I need hot water, now! Mary, hand me the rags."

Victoria rushed to the bedside and poured water into the basin. She gaped at Anne's huge swollen, blue-veined belly, and backed away. "I will fetch more water, Maggy."

"Mary, set the rags by the bed-stand and then take Henry and Sarah outside."

"Oh, indeed I will." She hurried from the room anxious to flee the terrible moans.

Thankfully, Anne's bed was sturdy. The headboard had slender wooden slats that she gripped, squeezing them as she writhed from one uncomfortable position to another.

"Mrs Whitmore," said Margaret folding a cloth, "if you need to bite down, this will help."

"Indeed, have you sent for my mother-in-law?" Her breathing heavy and laboured, sweat beaded on her upper lip.

"They are searching for her this very moment."

Margaret placed the rag in her mouth. Anne groaned, breathing through her nose.

"Bring more water," said Margaret. She dipped one of the rags in the basin, rung it out, and wiped Anne's belly.

Victoria rushed back carrying the hot kettle and refilled the basin.

"Here," Margaret handed the cloth to Victoria, "cleanse Mrs Whitmore as I have done." She whispered, "Now, Vic, I am going to look where the baby will come out. Its head may be coming out, don't cry and frighten Mrs Whitmore. You *must* stay calm."

She nodded. "Indeed, Maggy, I will."

"Very well then, Vic, because we need you."

Victoria affectionately placed her hand on Margaret's shoulder. "Aye, Margaret, I shall not leave your side. I will do whatever you wish me to."

"You are very brave, Vic. You won't be sorry. You and I are going to bring a baby into this world."

Victoria wiped her forehead on her sleeve, set her jaw, and watched intently as Margaret pulled the quilt away from Anne's legs.

"Cover her shoulders, Vic, Mrs Whitmore must not take a chill. Wipe her face, then help me set her legs."

"I am going to push your legs apart, Mrs Whitmore," said

Margaret in a calm tone. "I must see how far you are come with child. I have read many books on this, ma'am. I truly love medicine, and I am not afraid. Victoria and I will help you. Your mother will be here very soon."

She gently pushed Anne's knees apart. "Take hold of her ankles, Vic. Push her legs apart and back just a little. Hold her knees apart. There, Vic, see? See? Look, the baby's head is coming. Hold her knees apart Vic, the baby will be coming."

Margaret wiped the filmy mucus oozing from the birth canal.

Vicky leaned closer, whispering in awe, "That's its head?"

"Push now, Mrs Whitmore, push now. Bear down very hard," urged Margaret.

Victoria's eyes grew wider. "So those were the books you read so often late at night. No wonder you were always in the barnyard with the animals at birthing, and with Holly when she had puppies." Victoria swallowed hard "Oh, how proud I am of you, Sister."

Margaret nodded, not taking her eyes from Anne. "Oh, how proud *I am* of you Victoria, for you have not fainted. Keep pushing Mrs Whitmore!"

"Oh, where is Mother?" Anne thrashed, sweat dripped from her forehead, arms and legs.

"Keep her knees apart, Vic." Margaret stared wide-eyed at the baby's head while wiping away mucous and blood.

"See Vic, the head is now coming out faster; pretty soon the shoulders ..."

Victoria's brow furrowed. "Oh, yes, yes it is." She grimaced.

"Yes," said Margaret, "I am in wonder myself at this miracle: first the head and then the shoulders, and then the baby slides out wrapped in its slippery, shiny new skin. You'll see, you'll see."

Anne spit the cloth from her mouth, crying, "It's coming! It's coming!"

"Push, Mrs Whitmore, push! It's almost here."

Anne gripped the wooden slats; her knuckles white. She closed her eyes, writhing in pain, now whimpering quietly. She took a deep breath and bore down with all her strength.

"Just once more," cried Margaret, "its head is out; now the shoulders ... push!"

"I can't," screamed Anne, "for God's sake, pull it!"

Victoria jumped back in horror, closing her eyes. "Oh, no. Oh, no."

Margaret cradled the baby's dangling head, worrying more

at the anguish in Anne's pleading voice. "Vic, hold her knees apart."

With one last push, Anne felt the painful, yet easy gush as her baby slipped out of her body into Margaret's hands. Wiping the sweat from her face, she moaned, "Oh, God in heaven, thank you." She dashed away her tears and closed her eyes. "Oh, thank God, it's over."

"There now, baby," whispered Margaret as she held the watery, blood-covered newborn in her hands. The sisters' concentration was so great they didn't hear Granny Whitmore rush into the room. William, Lord Grayton, and Lizzy stood back, gaping in stunned wonder.

Granny Whitmore hurried to Margaret's side. "There's a girl. Turn her aside, dear. Now gently place your little finger inside her mouth and remove the matter." With a reassuring smile, she watched Margaret do it perfectly.

Still concentrating intently on the baby, Margaret nodded. "Thank you, ma'am." She glanced at Victoria. "Now, you must sever the umbilical cord, Vic. I shall hold her still."

Victoria swallowed hard. "Will the baby feel it, Maggy?"

Granny sighed. "Oh, my no."

Victoria took up the little knife and deftly severed the cord; her soft white hands calm and deliberate. "She's a beautiful little girl," she glowed at Anne.

"Now tie the string around it and make it snug, Miss Victoria," said Granny.

That being done, Margaret held the baby up with both hands. "Vic, wipe her clean while I hold her."

Margaret giggled as she turned the crying child over and over for her first bath. Victoria cleaned the blood and mucus from the child until she was a shiny, pink little mass of humankind.

Granny Whitmore stood back in awe. "Why, it looks as if you young ladies have done this a thousand times before."

Margaret looked up into Mrs Whitmore's face and smiled. "From now on I want nothing more in life but to deliver babies."

Victoria was enthralled with the baby's size. "Look, her little hands are no bigger than my thumb." She counted all fingers and toes. "A perfect form."

Granny Whitmore handed Margaret a cloth. "Put it under the loose umbilical cord and wrap the bellyband tight." That done, she handed the infant to Anne, who cradled the fussing child in her arms, kissing her face over and over.

Victoria quietly left the room and found her father, William,

Lizzy, Mary, Henry, and Sarah waiting just outside the door. Everyone had been weeping.

Lord Grayton put his arms around Victoria's shoulder. "Daughter, you look pale." He hugged her.

She smiled meekly. "I am but a little tired, Papa."

Together, Lizzy and Mary carried a chair to her side. "Here, Vic, you must sit."

The baby began to wail.

Victoria giggled. "She is a healthy little girl, Mr Whitmore."

William sighed. "Thank God, Lady Victoria. Thank you." He glanced at the closed door. "And my wife?"

"She is very very tired, but happy. You shall see for yourself."

Taking her father's hand, Victoria had tears in her eyes. "Oh, Papa, there are no words to explain what it feels like to bring a child into the world. Margaret did it all, Papa."

Just then Granny Whitmore came out, smiling. "William, Anne wishes to see you."

Rushing into the room, he hovered over her, kissing her brow. "You are safe. That is all I prayed for."

"Our daughter is beautiful, William, if it weren't for his lordship's daughters, I would not have survived. I would like to honour them. Please, I must speak to them."

William beckoned everyone come into the room. "Anne wishes to speak to you."

Everyone assembled around the bed.

Holding the infant in her arms, Anne's eyes glistened. "Lady Margaret, Lady Victoria, Lady Mary I have decided to name our daughter after you. I shall honour you both by calling her Margaret Mary Victoria."

The sisters nodded, both still in shock at what they had done. Holding hands, they approached the bed. "Mrs Whitmore," said Victoria, "I cannot tell you how thrilled I am at knowing this child will carry my name."

Margaret beamed. "I, too, am very honoured, Mrs Whitmore. I have learned a great lesson today, one I will carry with me for the rest of my life."

Mary so overcome with emotion, nodded.

Feeling left out, Lizzy wrinkled her nose. "What about me?"

Chapter 6 – Anne's Sister, Jane Stewart, Arrives

Jane Stewart left the Holybourne Orphanage unaware that her sister's baby had been born. She was in a very happy mood, for soon she would see Anne, and help deliver her second child. She felt assured that the vicar's wife, Mrs Connor, would do well at the orphanage in her stead, for she got on quite well with the children.

It was this same kindness from one of the farmers who lived nearby, old Thomas More, who offered Jane the rare opportunity to ride in his chaise to Alton. Jane gratefully accepted—precious few coins rattled about in her purse to pay a coach fare.

Mr More nodded. "I believe it to be my moral duty, Miss Jane, to help where I can at the orphanage." His old rheumy eyes could not find hers and yet he reassured her kindly, "I'm not fast anymore, but we'll get there all the same."

As his one-horse chaise descended the slope into the village of Alton, Jane's heart sank. She spied two strange carriages outside her sister's cottage. Fearing something dreadful, she hastily jumped. Her skirt caught on the broken, jagged-edged chaise-step and ripped a good portion of it away. Unaware, she hurried toward the cottage, her heart throbbing in her throat as she fought back tears.

Neighbours milled about the Whitmore cottage as she anxiously weaved in and around them. Finally reaching the cottage door, she entered, but found no one. Then she heard voices coming from a distant room. Quite suddenly a door opened, and to her utter amazement, Lord Grayton stepped out.

"My lord," in bewildered, shocked disbelief, Jane stepped back. Glancing around him, she caught a glimpse of Anne sitting in a chair, a bundle resting in her arms. William stood next to her, smiling. The entire room seemed to be filled with strangers.

"Oh, sister," she cried holding her hands to her face, "Oh, I thought something dreadful happened." She hurried to her side, dropping to her knees.

"Oh, Jane, I am very well. You must not worry, the baby came early."

Jane hugged her. "You are doing well? Yes, I can see for myself."

"Quite well, Sister. I am sorry for shocking you so. I thought you'd be here tomorrow."

Lord Grayton carried a chair for Jane. "Madam," he took her elbow, "please sit."

She curtsied, shocked that the Earl lowered himself to carry a chair for her. Glancing up, she smiled. "Thank you, my lord, how very kind of you."

Anne took her sister's hand. "Jane, you are looking pale and drawn."

"It is nothing, Anne." She coughed. "Just a cold, it shall pass."

William hemmed, "My lord, you remember Miss Stewart, my sister-in-law?"

The Earl took her hand to his lips. "So very nice to see you again, Miss Stewart." There came a long silence as the two gazed into each other's eyes.

Jane smiled. "Good morning, your lordship, I am honoured to be in your company, once again."

Lizzy giggled as she took hold of her father's arm. "Papa?"

He turned to find his daughters staring at him. "Daughters, meet Miss Stewart." He gestured for them to come closer. "Lady Margaret is my eldest, second is Victoria, Mary, and Elizabeth. Henry, of course, is my youngest, but then you knew that."

Each nodded. "Pleased to meet you, Miss Stewart," they said in unison.

Anne whispered over the sleeping baby, "Everyone, you may come now and peep at our angel. We have named her in honour of Lady Margaret, Lady Victoria, and Lady Mary. They delivered her, or else I should have died."

Lizzy's face drew up and said with a sigh, "Humph, they will name one of the pups after me."

Laughing, Henry pulled the blanket from the baby's face, running his finger over her cheek. Taking Sarah's hand, he whispered, "Look, Sarah, feel how soft she is."

"Indeed, my sister is pretty." She limped back to her little chair by the fire and sat, being quiet and inconspicuous; it was her nature.

"Indeed, my niece is a sweet child," Jane beamed. She

glanced up at Grayton's daughters. "Which of you is Lady Margaret, Mary and Victoria?"

The sisters stepped forward.

"I owe you a great debt of gratitude for saving my sister and my niece's life."

Grayton's chest swelled.

Margaret smiled. "I read many books, Miss Stewart." She glanced at her father. "Medicine has always been my passion."

"Indeed," said Lizzy, "Maggy is always the one to deliver pups and kittens. She even helped with Daisy, our milk cow."

"I had no idea," said her father, "why, Margaret, you never once told me of your passion for medicine."

"You have always been away, Papa. Mama forbade me to read such books."

"Well, obviously you read them anyway."

She smiled, sheepishly. "Indeed, Papa."

"Well, I am thankful you did," said Anne in gratefulness.

Lizzy stood in the back of the room unusually quiet, petting the family's very pregnant dog.

"And I," said Jane taking her sister's hand, "I shall forever be grateful to you ladies. And who is that child standing just there?" She gestured toward Lizzy.

"Oh, it is my youngest sister, Elizabeth," beamed Margaret. "Indeed, Miss Stewart it was Lizzy who saved the day. Without her finding Mrs Whitmore who knows what might have happened."

Lizzy's head came up, she smiled twiddling her fingers. "It was my duty, ma'am."

Grayton put his arms around her. "Indeed, Lizzy, I am very grateful to all of my daughters."

Finding Jane's leg to be exposed, he took up a quilt and covered it. "Your skirt, Miss Stewart."

Glancing down, she blushed. "Oh, I must have somehow ripped it."

Victoria whispered to Mary at how beautiful Miss Stewart is. "Indeed, and Papa has given her to blush." They giggled.

Granny Whitmore entered the room. "Well, I think it time Anne and the baby rest. I have cheese, wine, bread, and stew enough for everyone. Come now. We must leave Anne and William in peace."

Lord Grayton nodded at his daughters and followed them from the room.

Jane removed the quilt and stared down at her ripped frock.

"Oh, Anne, it is ruined, I can't possibly go."

"Take my Sunday frock. It hangs there on the peg."

Jane changed quickly, and while hurrying to Granny Whitmore's cottage, she noticed old Mr More, he was still driving his rickety old gig, but in circles. She sighed. *Probably all the while I've been in the cottage.*

She grabbed his horse by its bridle and stopped it. "Mr More, you must be hungry. Come join us for dinner. It is becoming dark, sir. I believe you and your horse need a rest."

His turtle-like little head swirled around his neck socket. "Ah, who's that?"

She reached for the frail, old man to help him down. Suddenly his lordship took his other arm. "There now, Miss Stewart, allow me to help."

"Thank you, my lord." She was astounded that he would lower himself to help a lowly old man. "Mr More's little body feels quite brittle, my lord."

"Sir, put your feet steady on the ground," he said.

With a wrinkled frown, Mr More squinted. "Whose deep voice do I hear, commanding in such a tone?"

"Lord Grayton here to help you, Mr More." He held gently to the spry old fellow. He could feel through the old man's worn clothes his sharp bones. "Easy does it."

"Lord who?"

Jane smiled at his lordship. "Thank you, sir."

"Not to worry, Miss Stewart, we each, in our turn, grow infirm. Let us hope more in the world are of your kind nature."

Her face grew pink. "Aye, my lord, and the world would be without need if they were all like you." She felt his warm eyes gaze softly upon her face, and it felt lovely.

As they approached Granny's cottage, William opened the door. Warm, yellow candlelight spilt out onto their path. Making their way in the small, but neat cottage, they found only four chairs at the table. The Grayton sisters, Henry and Sarah, sat like Turks on the floor, making a half circle about the warm fire. They politely awaited their portions of stew.

Granny excused herself. "I shall take a bowl to William and Anne. I won't be long."

Lizzy jumped up. "I shall help you, Mrs Whitmore."

Grayton stared at his youngest daughter in disbelief.

"Well," said Granny wiping her hands on her apron, "thank you, child, indeed, that would please me."

Lizzy carefully lifted the large pot from the triangle iron that hung over the flames, being careful, for it was heavy. Granny stuffed chunks of bread in her apron pockets.

Henry took the pot from her. "I'll help you, Lizzy, it's much too heavy."

"I'll hold the door," said Sarah moving alongside him.

The three, in cautious steps, left the cottage.

To Grayton's utter amazement Margaret, Mary and Victoria passed along bowls, spoons and mugs. *And to think not quite so long ago they were such selfish self-centred little prigs. Such wonders ... I can hardly understand this transformation.* He remained in awe as he watched his family being polite and considerate. His heart was truly touched.

When Granny returned, she took hands around the table and offered a blessing.

Grayton took Jane's hand and gazed upon her silent face. Through her callouses, he felt her warmth and felt pity for her. It had been a long year since the passing of his wife, Elizabeth, and his heart was stirring; he was unhappy and unsettled. As well, it had been many years since the passing of his father. *But, am I really free after all?*

Was it the constant London society that quite spent his nerves or the lavishly attired and witty ladies who were always *wanting* at his side? He abhorred the idleness of those dames and would find himself longing for the freedom of his beloved Rosewood Park, away from London and its artificiality, its haughty vulgar laughs and sneers. But, his daughters and son needed the proper upbringing ... *no, I am not really free at all.*

Still holding Miss Stewart's hand, he felt the strength of his body tighten. He knew when he first visited the Holybourne Orphanage months ago that she had the power to control his heart. Her beauty radiated. *I want her loveliness stirring within my heart. I can barely stand to touch her calloused, neglected hand for want of pulling her out of this wretched life.* His breathing quickened, suddenly he felt her hand move slightly and he opened his eyes. Everyone about the table was patiently waiting for him. He hastily blurted, "Amen."

Chapter 7 – A Great House is to be Built for Jane

A year passed between Lord Grayton and Miss Jane Stewart. He thoughtfully continued to have his footman gather Anne's letters to Jane and deliver them to the orphanage. Indeed, why not, his carriage passed there almost daily. To deliver a letter would be no trouble.

Grayton had been thinking long and hard about his desire for the beautiful Miss Stewart. She was indeed poor, without connections, social affiliations, and he knew the cruel snobbery of his society and what they would think of her, what they would do to her if he would have any association with such a woman.

As well, he thought of his daughters and what an alliance with Miss Stewart would bring to their aspirations to marry well; he thought of Henry and his entailment, Rosewood Park, the London holdings. His son had to marry well and have sons of his own. What sort of example would he set for taking such a woman as Miss Stewart? He was tormented, his body ached. He even weighed the idea of taking her as a mistress, but the shadow of her smile would surely haunt him, and he knew the power of such a woman. *No, I cannot do such a thing.*

No, he thought better of his weakness and made his mind up to forget her, entirely. Indeed, he convinced himself that he must stay in control. To test his new resolve this very morning, he would deliver Anne's letter to Miss Stewart himself. *I shall overcome this.*

When his carriage stopped in front of the orphanage, he stepped down, took in a great breath, and dismissed his footman. "I shall deliver the letters myself, Johnson."

Grayton made his way through the muddy path careful to step on the meagre few stones placed there for such a path. "Indeed, a pitiful sight," he scoffed, "as if some sort of pitiful pathway." He fussed at the mud already seeping into his boots, but even the mud, the small slabs of broken stone, the airy chill about his neck, nay, none of these obstacles deterred him. He felt the power to confront her gather strength, his worries abated. He was capable and eager as he stepped upon each wobbly step. *I shall prevail.*

When he tried the knob, the door suddenly opened. There stood Miss Stewart, smiling. "Good afternoon, my lord."

Her light blue eyes poured into his heart. His body tightened; warmth moved from his feet to his brow, heat twiddled his fingers. He knew he had made a mistake. *It seems I am not quite ready yet.* He swallowed many times to bring moisture to his parched throat. "Good afternoon Miss Stewart." He turned and looked out over the uneven green hedgerows, "Lovely day."

"Very," she looked out over the pile of broken rain buckets, "a bit rainy perhaps. Would you come in, my lord?"

"Thank you, Miss Stewart." He followed, taking in her lovely scent. She brushed by him closing the door. His knees grew weak. *Control yourself,* he thought over and over. "I have long been absent, Miss Stewart." He chose his words slowly and carefully.

She nodded. "Indeed, my lord."

Now clearing his throat, he squeaked, "I have long been absent ..." his breathing increased, "yes, I have not collected your sister's posts myself, having my footman gather them. You must have noticed?"

"Yes, my lord, you remained in the carriage at each visit here. If it pleases you, sir, my sister and I will post our own letters. I sense we have worn out our welcome." She nervously picked at her fingernails. "Surely we have taken advantage of your good nature."

"Oh, no, Miss Stewart, that is not ... why, there is no trouble in stopping, I assure you." He felt miserable at seeing her happy face melt into sadness. He closed his eyes trying to take back control of his body, his breathing. *I am not ready for this.* He admonished his weak flesh as he reached for her; he had to touch her, hold her. Suddenly the cries of a child pierced the moment. "God in heaven," he jolted, "who is that?"

A child ran into the vestibule, and his lordship instinctively took her up into his arms. "Oh, my, your foot is bleeding." He sat her on the window-seat and removed his handkerchief. "Well, now, I see a little accident here." He wrapped her bleeding foot.

"Oh, dear me," Jane frowned. "I shall be back, sir. Please make yourself at home, sir." She picked up the little girl and hurried from the room.

Grayton remained standing in the vestibule, such as it was,

and for the first time he noticed how impoverished the house was. How overworked Miss Stewart looked. He wondered why he had not noticed all this before. "After all," he said aloud as he glanced around, "I have made many visits to this old house before, and I should have noticed its disrepair and the squalor." He breathed through his mouth.

He walked around the makeshift sitting room and noticed the walls—dingy, cracked and sallow in colour. The ceiling, at this minute, dripped rainwater. The stains on the floor were many, and the entry door did not keep the raw wind from blowing in.

"Dear me," he said aloud, becoming increasingly agitated, "who should live here, I should like to know!" And the thought of how sickly pale Miss Stewart had become. "Miss Stewart, where are you?"

One of the children, a scraggly-haired little urchin, curled around the door and stepped into the room "She's in the kitchen, sir. Follow me."

His lordship trailed behind the barefoot little boy and soon found Jane washing the little girl's cut foot.

"I am sorry for the bloody handkerchief, my lord. I shall wash it and return it to you tomorrow."

He looked at the little girl and smiled. "See there little one, from now on you must wear your boots. Let that be a lesson to you." He stood erect feeling the power of sage advice echo about the room.

But the little girl just stared at him.

"Dear me, Miss Stewart, did I say something wrong?"

"She has no boots, sir. None of the children do." Jane hugged the little girl and lifted her down.

He felt his sage advice sink to his stomach. "Oh, well, then ..." and his voice withered into nothingness. His mind teetered along the venue of blight. He turned suddenly and just before leaving the room stopped. "Miss Stewart, I must say, you look unwell."

"Ah, no, my lord, I do not think I am unwell."

"Yes, well I have noticed a cough interrupting your words. I have a mind to bring Margaret with me next visit next ... I believe you are in need of rest. Is there not one other person who may relieve you here, even for a day?"

"Oh, no, my lord, there is no one else but me and Fanny, the cook. Occasionally, the vicar's wife, Mrs Connor, comes when I visit with my sister, Anne, but lately Mrs Connor has not offered, and I have not had the luxury of rest. There are twenty children to clothe and feed, my lord. And now poor old Mr More is about the orphanage more and more, bless him. He tries to help. However, he is only fit to keep the fires burning. But I ask no more of him; he has quit his home it seems, and has no other place to sleep."

"Well, my next visit ... tomorrow it will be, I shall bring my daughter Margaret. We shall then devise a plan."

A plan? Looking astonished, she studied his face, unsure of what provoked the outburst.

"I must be going," he said. "Goodbye."

"Indeed, my lord."

Stepping up into the carriage, he grumbled to his footman. "That woman is incapable of turning away a stray dog, and she will surely die at their mercy."

"Yes, sir."

Grayton thought of nothing but Miss Stewart the entire ride back to Rosewood Park. Within minutes of arriving home, he summoned Margaret to join him in the study.

"Yes, Papa, you wanted to see me?"

"Margaret, tomorrow morning, we shall ride to the Holy-bourne Orphanage and visit with Miss Stewart. I just left there, and I am indeed shocked at the appalling squalor and conditions she and the children endure. I want you to think upon the matter. Miss Stewart looks very ill, indeed."

She watched her father pace back and forth in front of the hearth fire as if trying to solve an insurmountable problem. She had never seen him so worried and fretful. "Of course, Papa, I shall think upon the matter." She was not exactly sure what she was to think about, and wisely concluded, *I will know more to-morrow—when I visit this orphanage that Papa speaks of.*

Lord Grayton trusted Margaret. He knew how astute and mindful she was at medicine and fixing broken bones, tending the ill. After all, the continual well-being of the barn animals was proof enough, and how wonderfully successful she was at mending the cuts and wounds of the help. Many of the villagers came to her when the apothecary was too busy for them. She always obliged them, eager for the challenge, saddened when failure won out, but Margaret would then go again to her books and learn more from her failures. Never would she let a death or a complication sway her determination to see a healing.

She interrupted her father's deep thought, "Papa, may I be excused, sir? If we are to be up at first light, I must sleep now, and you the same."

"Yes, my dear." He kissed her brow. "You may be excused."

Margaret stood very still as his arms dropped to his side.

"Papa, that was the very first time you have ever kissed me good-night." Tears welled in her eyes.

He looked at her, stunned. "I, I had no idea. Forgive me, Margaret. I will try to be a better father."

"You already are, Papa." She left, quietly closing the door behind her.

As she made her way to her room, Victoria stuck her head around her door. "Psst, Margaret, what is wrong with Papa?"

"Nothing, why do you ask?"

"When he came home tonight he passed me in the hall. I greeted him, but he didn't see me, even as I stood directly in his path."

"He *is* troubled, Victoria. Tomorrow I am to go with him to the orphanage in Holybourne to see the matter first hand. I do believe Mrs Whitmore's sister, Miss Stewart, is very ill."

"Oh, my. Well, if anyone can save her, it shall be you, Margaret."

* * *

The next morning Grayton and Margaret set off for the orphanage. Along the way, he commented about the deplorable conditions of the orphanage, the children, and Miss Stewart.

Margaret listened, occasionally looking over at her troubled father. Clearly, he was in love with this woman, Miss Stewart.

The carriage ambled up to the old weather-beaten house with its warped steps and broken windows. The old, once-grand mansion had grown into a grey, dilapidated, haggish bit of history. A shudder went through Margaret, and it seems her father felt the same chill. She took his hand. "Come along Papa."

When they entered the dark, dank old place, Margaret immediately had the urge to throw open the few windows and doors and let in the healing warmth of the sun. She noticed a few of the older children had stopped in their tracks and were watching them with trepidation. *They probably think we are here to take one of them.*

"Oh, Papa, how is it these children live in such squalor? Cannot we at least provide a clean, dry home for them – with a warm kitchen and helpers? Miss Stewart cannot do all this with just a cook, with no servants. It is no wonder she looks ill."

Just then a door opened, and an older woman curtsied in its threshold. "Good morn, I'm Fanny, the cook. Miss Jane told us you'd be here." She looked them up and down.

Margaret felt self-conscious in her fine clothes when poverty was all around her at every scene.

"Miss Jane will be down shortly. Can I bring tea?"

"No, Fanny, thank you," said his lordship. "We had tea just a short time ago. We shall wait here for Miss Stewart."

Within a very few minutes, Jane entered the room. She smiled at his lordship, colouring deeply.

His knees trembled.

Margaret took her hand. "Good afternoon, Miss Stewart. Papa tells me you are not feeling well."

Jane dabbed her lips with her pocket handkerchief. "Why, I am but a little tired Lady Margaret, that is all."

After a brief conversation with her, Margaret concluded by all her questions and observations that Jane was not ill in a diseased way, but only exhausted and near collapse with worry for the well-being of the orphans. She also noticed an old man wandering about the rooms as if he were lost.

Jane followed Margaret's eyes. "I cannot turn him out, poor old fellow. Mr More has forgotten his way home."

"There now, Miss Stewart, rest your mind. I have a plan." Margaret turned to her father. "Papa, once you complete the new road in Alton, we must build a new house to replace this old one. I could continue to study medicine here, and Miss Stewart could keep and shelter her young ones in decency. You know very well, Papa, that she will never turn away a child or the elderly. Rather than being sent to London with Aunt Catherine, I should love to manage medicine here with Miss Stewart."

Jane remained motionless, too stunned for words.

"Hmm." Grayton straightened his shoulders and walked across the old spongy, wood-rotted floor to the window. When he parted the heavy, tattered drapes, he overheard a muffled cough from somewhere about his boots. Looking down, he found, there huddled behind the drape, a small child. He lifted him up muttering something about his thin little arms, and how cold they felt. He glanced at his daughter and Miss Stewart. His heart rose in his throat. "I am trapped by women and children!" He smiled down into the urchin's face and took his chin. "Well then, little one, where shall this Great House be built?"

Margaret and Jane ran to him, both laughing and crying. Margaret kissed his cheek.

Jane kissed his forehead and then suddenly pulled back in stunned disbelief, embarrassed at being so forward with his lordship. "Excuse me, my lord." But she could no longer deny the esteem and affection she felt for him.

He looked pleasantly surprised at such an innocent display of affection and nodded his approval. His face flushed—Jane Stewart kissing him for the first time was exhilarating; he knew it would not be the last.

Margaret took Jane's hand. "Look, Papa, look at her this very minute. Miss Stewart has colour in her cheeks, her smile is come back. Indeed, her worry over the children has been settled.

He nodded. *Miss Stewart's worries are over, mine however, seem to be just beginning. How shall I ever recover from her lips on my brow?*

He was thankful for his daughter's lively banter as his heart was still pounding; he was at a loss for words. However, he regained his composure, slightly. With a flush still on his face, he spoke in a very soft tone. "Miss Stewart, my family and I shall, again, call in the morning. There are many things to discuss for the new orphanage. Good afternoon."

Tears of happiness gleamed in her eyes. She waved from the door. "Good afternoon my lord," she whispered, still swimming in the euphoria of kissing him.

Chapter 8 – Love Works its Power

Jane Stewart was clearly shaken at the astounding turn of events of Lord Grayton's announcement just yesterday. That very next morning, as she sat alone in deep meditation under her favourite shade tree, his lordship came to her, alone. He found her head bowed and gently tapped her shoulder.

She calmly looked up into his eyes and stood. Without a word, she traced the sweetness of his bold and handsome face with her fingertips. Such tenderness only a butterfly could make. She then lovingly closed his eyes with her lips and kissed his mouth.

Grayton's daughters stood at the garden window in awe as their father returned the kiss.

"Well now, sisters," said Margaret, "I do believe we should be about some other window." She took Lizzy's hand and hastily led them into the kitchen. Fanny was preparing breakfast.

"Oh, well now, how nice. Are you staying to eat?" asked Fanny.

"Oh, no, thank you, Fanny. We are on our way to Alton. Father had a message to deliver to Miss Stewart. He should soon be joining us, and we'll be on our way."

Holding a smile, Fanny glanced out the window, again. "Ah, yes, of course."

* * *

On the ride to Alton, where his lordship was to announce to the Whitmores the new orphanage project, he was very quiet. Occasionally a smile would come about his mouth. His eyes held a look quite foreign to the girls.

Lizzy nudged Mary, Mary nudged Victoria.

Margaret glared at all three, finally whispering warmly, "Leave him to his dreams, will you."

The sisters shrugged and resumed their idle, sisterly clack.

The rumbling carriage, the horses' leather-grind, and the stomping of hooves brought Henry and Sarah immediately into the yard. With outstretched arms, they stood in glee.

Everyone gathered in the Whitmores' sitting room while Grayton made the announcement of the new orphanage. That bit of astounding news put everyone in ecstasy.

His lordship decided, there on the spot, that a new orphanage should be built sooner rather than waiting to complete the road. "Both feats certainly can be done at the same time, I should think. William. I am quite certain you can oversee the progress of a road and a new orphanage. Since I dare say, the children cannot stand another winter in such conditions."

William's mouth dropped, but he quickly recovered. "Oh, yes, my lord, indeed, I shall be honoured. And I agree, the little mites have suffered long enough, not one more winter in such conditions, indeed, my lord, not one more winter. And what of this grand orphanage that is to be built, sir? Do you have a plan for its size and worth?"

"Spare not a pound, William. It should be grand and warm; definitely warm and dry. And the house should have a large kitchen. Each room is to be furnished with many chairs and sofas. There should be ample fireplaces and rooms enough for many servants. There will be special quarters for Miss Stewart so that her new library and personal chambers are more than comfortable, without need of one single thing. Perhaps my daughters and your good wife, Anne, should help plan the estate. I dare say, Miss Stewart would never indulge herself. Yes, I want a very dear place for her, a home with many windows that look out upon the meadows and pastures where she may, in turn, fill up on its grandeur and power as I do."

His daughters sat in amused silence.

Indeed, thought Margaret, *father is very much in love with her. I cannot blame him, though, for Miss Stewart is truly a compassionate woman. I cannot wait until I come under her power of kindness when working with those little waifs.*

When the Graytons left, Anne and William stood in the side-yard waving good-bye.

"William, is all this but a dream? Well, I simply *must* go visit with Jane morning next. Who could have guessed at such a miracle as this?"

"Such a miracle indeed, Anne. Now I am to oversee many things that bring such happiness to so many people. Though the Earl is a man of wealth, he is a very good man ... it is truly beyond my reasoning at these turn of events."

Anne smiled at the naivety of her husband. "I think his lord-ship is very much in love with my sister."

William looked astonished. "Why, Anne, why would you say such a thing?"

Chapter 9 – Margaret's Invention

During the long drive home from Alton, Margaret watched Henry fall into a deep sleep. She also noticed that her father was unusually quiet as he stared out at the early evening sky. It was quiet, this ride home. She thought over the important decisions her father had so recently made and pondered the accomplishments wealth and privilege could bring. She thought of the love he surely felt for Miss Stewart and wondered, as well, if he even knew. Margaret was certain Miss Stewart loved him in return—it was in her eyes, after all. Why, the very way she kissed his lips under the apple tree was beyond anything she had read in books.

Margaret was overwhelmed by his generosity and prayed he would find his way—that he would find his heart. She closed her eyes half-listening to her sister's banter when quite unexpectedly a vision of Sarah came to mind. She thought it a pity that she suffered so from her leg deformity and often thought how sad that her back ached so. *Surely there must be a way to ease such pain.*

Upon arriving at Rosewood Park, there was little chatter as everyone stepped from the carriage yawning and stretching. It had been a long day. After a late dinner, everyone settled into their rooms and the Great House of Rosewood Park grew quiet.

The next morning Margaret awoke from a troubling dream, but could remember only small flashes of it … crippled people, dogs running, crowds of people milling about. She could not put any order to it, but her heart was sad, and she felt a compelling reason to once more read on matters of the crippled—like Sarah.

She filled many days in the library contemplating Sarah's bad leg. Suddenly she had a flash. "But, of course, I shall fit her with a harness, like I fashioned for Mary's dog when it broke its leg. She jumped from her chair and hurried into her father's study to share her idea, but he was not there. Just then the door opened.

"Where is Father, Maggy?" said Henry.

Margaret took his hands and twirled him around. "Oh, I have a plan, Henry—a plan that Sarah will walk just like us, no longer hobbling. Come and help me."

"Make her walk? What do you mean by such a thing?"

"Come with me, Henry. She took his hand. "Come, you'll soon see."

* * *

When Lord Grayton entered his study, he stopped abruptly. "What in Heaven's name ..."

Henry grinned. "Papa, look how Sarah will walk like us." He walked up and down the room with the odd contraption strapped to his body.

Margaret stood holding two long leather straps, some old shoe buckles, some twine. "Indeed, Papa, I have fashioned a device to Henry's leg, an experiment, if you will."

"What sort of device, Margaret?"

"Here, Papa, let me show you." She adjusted the straps and tightened a few buckles. "There now that should do it." She winked at Henry with a giggle. "Very well, brother, show Papa."

"By God, that is the very device you rigged for the dog when he broke his leg. Sarah will not know what to make of it. Dear me, we must not waste a minute more. Come, we must go to her this very minute."

Henry clapped his hands. "Oh, Papa, I cannot wait to see her little face. It will shine like the sun."

"Oh, indeed, Henry." He turned to Margaret. "Daughter, what a grand idea of yours."

"Oh, it was just a matter of time that someone would have thought of such a thing, Papa."

* * *

That very morning, just as Anne glanced out the window, Lord Grayton's carriage clamoured up the lane. "Dear me, they are come very early this morning. Oh, come look, William, *all* the girls are with him as well."

When the horses came to a stop, Henry was first out, shouting excitedly as he ran to the door calling for Sarah.

"Oh, Mr Whitmore," said Margaret, "we have such a surprise for Sarah that you will hardly believe your eyes."

Lizzy, Mary and Victoria nodded, tittering and giggling.

Grayton had a grin on his face. "William, Margaret has a great surprise for little Sarah. She invented a wonderful contraption ... of sorts. One that, I must say, will undoubtedly change her life forever."

"My lord?" said William, looking puzzled. "What sort of a miracle? How many more miracles could you, or your family, possibly bestow upon us now?"

"You shall see, William, you shall see. Let us go inside that we may witness it at once."

"Certainly, come in, please, my lord."

Henry took Sarah's hand. "Sarah, you will not believe it, even with your own eyes."

"Henry, you must not tease me. Tell me at once what you are about."

"Sarah, we have a wonderful surprise for you—wonderful," said Grayton.

Sarah, quiet and shy, stood before him, pulling Henry alongside her. "Yes, my lord."

"Henry, make a little room in front of the hearth and set the box there," said Margaret.

William and Anne exchanged glances.

Henry took Sarah's hand. "Come along, Sarah."

Margaret busily assembled the leather straps into the metal loops while Henry held the metal rods.

Growing more and more apprehensive, Sarah backed up, shaking her head. "I don't know ..."

"Come on, Sarah, don't be afraid. Remember Willie when he broke his leg and Maggie made a sling for his leg? Well, soon you will see. Come now," he whispered, "I won't let anything happen to you, I promise."

"Very well, Henry."

Margaret giggled as she took Sarah's hand. "Not to worry, our dear little friend." She held up the straps and buckles. "All of these things have been made especially for you. We have an experiment, if you don't mind, Sarah. I promise not one thing shall hurt you."

Sarah examined the leather straps and buckles. "I cannot imagine what you are going to do with these things."

Henry squeezed her hand. "No need to worry, Sarah."

Just then Granny Whitmore hurried into the cottage. "Forevermore, I was so worried when I noticed all the Graytons have come. I dressed as soon as I could," she said catching her breath. "Is anything wrong?"

"Not to worry, Mother, we are all in amazement at what Lady Margaret has fashioned. It's a miracle for Sarah—a device she invented."

Laying the leather straps with buckles and knots, pieces of wood and cloth, black metal rods of all lengths in front of her, she gestured to Sarah. "Come, come, Sarah. Henry, help her stand straight."

Margaret fitted one strap around Sarah's waist. Two metal rods with wood bracing were attached to her thigh; her deformed leg cradled in a stirrup. The device was now resting squarely on the floor. Fussing with the buckles and straps, she was finally satisfied it would hold Sarah's weight. Sitting back, she nodded to Henry. "Let her stand free."

Sarah nervously glanced up at her mother, who nodded with an approving smile.

William held out his hands. "Come, Sarah."

Her eyes widened, she swallowed hard. Glancing down at her leg, she moved an inch. "I will, Papa." Balancing herself, she gingerly put her weight onto the device. Inch by inch she moved toward her father. "Papa, it doesn't hurt," she marvelled, "it doesn't hurt to walk anymore." Moving slowly, she smiled. "My back doesn't hurt, Mama."

Henry took her hand. "Come along, Sarah."

"Sarah, this will take some getting used to. I am afraid you will not be able to run. Well, not yet at least, but with a few changes here and there, and as you naturally grow accustomed to it, we shall just see what comes of it," said Margaret.

"Thank you, Lady Margaret, thank you," said Sarah.

Looking over to her father, she smiled. "Dare I believe that studying medicine is where I shall truly find my purpose in life, Papa?"

Chapter 10 – Rosewood Park

After their return from the Whitmores,' Lord Grayton summoned Margaret to join him in his study.

She entered quietly and found him at his desk. "Yes, Papa, you sent for me?"

"Sit by the fireside for a moment, my dear. I am near finished with some business."

"Certainly, Papa." She sat in her favourite chair—an old, overstuffed chaise lounge, her Papa's favourite as well. She relaxed in its softness as the fire's heat permeated her every muscle. Falling into a philosophical sort of mood, she looked at him and felt a great sadness. *Surely he is lonely without Mother. And then the flailing possibility of a future with Miss Stewart, obviously he is deeply in love with her. But her station in life is so beneath ours. What a wicked turn for him.* She sighed heavily.

He looked up. "Well now, daughter, what was that all about?"

"With all the joy today at the Whitmores,' I was in wonder of *your* happiness Father, that is all."

He studied her for a moment. "Margaret, I called for you, my little *miracle worker*, to congratulate you on your successful invention for Sarah, and to tell you how very proud I am of you. I didn't call you here to discuss *my* happiness."

"But, Papa, you are always alone and sad. I can see it in your eyes. Even today, at your happiest moment watching Sarah, your thoughts were miles away, your heart was miles away. I am only sorry that I cannot help you, sir."

His shoulders drooped; his chin met his chest. "No, Margaret, you cannot help me. I dare say no one can help me."

She pressed her hand to her heart. "I understand, Papa, I truly do. Perhaps you shall find a way after all." She stood. "It is not only I who understands your predicament regarding Miss Stewart ... we all do, Mary, Victoria and Lizzy. I don't suppose Henry is aware. So, do not underestimate us, sir."

"Indeed not." He gently kissed her forehead. "I shall be at breakfast in the morning, good night, Margaret."

"Very well, Papa." With a sad smile, she left the room.

His lordship traversed the long hall toward his bedchamber and stopped. *My children seem ignorant when it comes to my marriage eligibility. Oh, I suppose from the perspective of a young heart, class distinction, rank, and privilege mean nothing, but one my age, simply cannot marry so decidedly beneath one's self, someone without proper connections, wealth, and family. They have no idea that an imprudent arrangement between Miss Stewart and me would bring shame to them. Our relatives would be mortified at the very thought. I must think of my children's futures, for who should associate with such a family if I took Jane for my wife.*

A dark shadow seemed to pervade his entire body. *Eh, gads, I sound like my father.* He wiped his eyes feeling trapped and helpless. *But I cannot betray my family—they must marry well. I must find a way to stay a great distance from Miss Stewart.*

His shoulders slumped, feeling doomed, he sighed heavily. *I will speak with Margaret in the morning, and eventually the children. No doubt my actions and associations, my overly familiar association with my tenants has presented an entirely wrong message to them.*

Now in his room, he stood in front of his hearth rubbing his hands. *I will take my family to London and escape the country life for a while, at least a year. Surely by then my daughters will be exposed to proper society and refreshed. Yes, it will be beneficial for them to mingle with their own kind. Henry dares all things exciting, London shall keep him enticed. And it is time for his formal education, Eton shall do quite nicely.*

He thought about his children's aunt, Lady Catherine. *Indeed, she has been urging me to bring them back into the proper social circles. 'Bring them back to London society ... the sooner the better, John.'* She had insisted so often.

She is right thought Grayton, damning himself. *I should have listened to her long ago. I shall inform the children we will leave for London soon. And, as well, I will see to it first off that Whitmore is settled in the business about the new road and the new orphanage.*

As he closed the latest chapter in his life—excluding the woman he loved so passionately and the summer fields of green he so desperately needed to survive, his beloved Rosewood Park—his heart grew heavier. To leave behind all the kind and loving people in Alton carried a terrible price to pay for the proper social standing his family absolutely had to maintain.

Grayton had made his decision as he stood at the fireside unaware of morning's first light inching its way into his room. The once red sizzling embers had turned into a soft grey ash, the room grew very cool, but he hardly noticed the chill as he dressed for breakfast.

During the meal, there was happy conversation from his family. They were all still very much in high spirits from the day before with little Sarah and her new walking device.

Elizabeth glanced over at her father. "Papa, are you feeling unwell this morning? You have not spoken two words."

He remained sullen and distant. The room grew quiet.

Mary and Victoria stopped their sisterly chatter. Henry stopped playing with his food. Margaret laid her silver down. They watched him.

Grayton sipped the last of his coffee. Now standing, he nodded to Margaret. "Daughter, I wish to speak with you in the library, but first finish your breakfast, dear."

"Very well, Papa, I am finished."

With that they both excused themselves, leaving Henry and his sisters at the table in wonder. Victoria and Mary whispered, "Hurry to the floor grate, we can listen to them there!"

As Grayton entered the library, he took in the familiar scent of the old leather-bound ex libris. The heavy, dark-red velvet window coverings were pulled back. It was a damp morning, a bright grey day exposing the room's quietness.

The hearth lay empty as Grayton approached. Sniffing the cold ash, he rubbed his nose, "a bit musty." He tugged the rope pull. "Hall shall have it going in no time, my dear. Please, Margaret, take a seat."

"Go on, Papa."

"I have a mind to return to London, Margaret ... all of us. I expect not to return to Rosewood Park for a least a year." He turned away, clasping his hands behind his back staring out the window.

Margaret leaned forward. "Papa, what do you mean? We have finally come together as a family, and you are now to pull us apart? What is the meaning? I cannot make out what your plan is about. I dare say, for once I am truly happy here."

"*You* are truly happy ..."

"Beg pardon my lordship, you rang, sir?" said Hall.

Grayton gestured toward the hearth. "The fire, Hall ..."

"Oh, indeed, my lord." The servant began his business of building a fire.

Grayton turned toward his daughter, but her words cut him short. "Victoria and Mary are not squabbling at each other, peace has come between them, and Lizzy is so very happy with Granny Whitmore, her French is wonderful. And Henry has grown so dear. The Whitmores are good enough, and what of the new road Papa? And what about Miss Stewart? Are you to leave all this for London's society? I cannot reason, Papa, your meaning?"

"Margaret, you must understand, I am an Earl ..."

"Even Queen Charlotte smiles upon our world here, Papa. Her children romp and play wild and free with us. And the King always comments at being comfortable and at ease—away from London society. His very words at his last visit, 'I cannot rest in such affability and calmness anywhere else in England as I do here – this is a sanctuary.' "

But she could see her father's determined look. Indeed, his mind was made up. She knew he was beyond reasoning; her heart wrenched.

"Margaret dear, forgive me, but you must trust me. You are still very young, and do not know the ways of society. If I should die, this estate, our London home and all my wealth are entailed to Henry—that is the material point. If, God forbid, something should happen to him you girls would be left with nothing. You must mingle in the proper society and marry well. I am afraid I have left you all with too much freedom. And now I am to suffer for it too. Yes, suffer even more than you realise."

He thought of his beautiful Jane and closed the thought as quickly. "Grieve not a moment longer, Margaret. I need you desperately to help with the others. I need your strength, daughter. I cannot do this alone. I wish this of you ... to understand and to trust me." He sat down next to her and dropped his head in his hands.

Margaret tried to understand her father ... this kind, yet troubled man that he had become. The sadness that enveloped his heart was hard for her to endure. She *felt* his meaning. After all, if she and her sisters *were* left penniless the novelty of freedom, the novelty of cold, dirty housing, the novelty of helping the less fortunate would stare them in the face—they would become *one of them*. She was confused and disgusted with her own double standard of thinking.

Wiping her eyes, she took his hand. "Papa dear, I do understand the situation we are in, and I am sorry over it. You have tried to do the right thing. I suppose we must leave Rosewood Park, although I, and I am quite sure my sisters and Henry will never be the same nor as happy ever again in our lives. We must explain this to them now, and I will help you, Papa, but you shall never remove the country from our hearts."

"Nor would I want it so, Margaret." He wiped his eyes. "Thank you, dear. I am grieved beyond words to leave my beloved Rosewood Park—where my very soul lives. However, time will pass, and we shall return."

"I know, Papa, but I shall worry for your health. Promise me you will keep your strength and good spirits. I am worried that those in London will swallow you up."

"Now, now, Margaret, I dare say what an imagination you have for such a young woman. Who shall swallow me up? Do not worry, child." But he knew exactly what his daughter meant. He patted her on the head. "So, come now, shall we be strong together? Let us speak with the others. We must convince them that their future happiness lies in London."

* * *

Early on, after the family left Rosewood Park to live in their London townhouse, Grayton found that Margaret's passion for practising medicine and the caring for children would not be denied. She grew quite melancholy and often lamented that she would go quite mad if not about helping the sick. He finally consented to her returning to the orphanage.

He promised that she could stay for two months, return home to London and then he would decide her fate. She was, as well, not to temp or tantalise her sisters or brother at her freedom.

Margaret was overjoyed at the prospect. "Oh, Papa, I feel as if I am a captive bird set free."

Over tea with Lady Catherine, his lordship announced his decision regarding Margaret's future. She would be allowed to return to the orphanage, but only after the new one was completed. Lady Catherine was speechless at such an idea.

"After all, my dear Catherine, you have Mary, Victoria, Elizabeth and Henry in your nest, and, I might add, a very handsome sum in the bargain. I will not have a single word more discussed over the matter. I have left a good portion of the discipline and guidance of my children to you, and now you must be satisfied with that."

"Oh, indeed, my lord I am, I am. It is just that ..."

"No more, madam." Grayton straightened his shoulders, his black eyes glared at her. "No more."

Silence enveloped the room.

Along with this troubling decision to let Margaret return to Holybourne, he chose *not* to visit her there, she must come to London. An encounter with Miss Stewart's beautiful eyes would certainly do him in. Not an evening ended that did not have *her* face upon his pillow.

Chapter 11 – The Whitmores – Alton, Five Years Hence

"Mummy, I shall walk to the road to welcome Aunt Jane," said Sarah all a breath. She was quite excited to visit with her aunt and stay at the orphanage for a month full. She had grown tall for her age of ten and five and held herself quite graceful—she grew adept at wearing the device.

Her favourite companion (next to her Aunt Jane, of course) was the dear Lady Margaret. Indeed, it was she who first piqued her interest in books and found Sarah an intelligent young girl; her appetite for books was voracious, no matter the subject, she simply loved to learn all things new. Her favourite presents were books, and her favourite pastime at the Holybourne Orphanage was being left to read to the children in the great library.

Sarah always looked forward to visiting the orphanage, and this morning as she stood anxiously awaiting her aunt's arrival, her attention was suddenly thrust upon the narrow, twisting roadway just ahead. There, finally, she spied her aunt's chaise as it rumbled down the slight approach to their lane.

"She is come, Mama."

"Very well, Sarah," called her mother. "Remember, be very quiet, Margaret Victoria is ill with cold, and she is sleeping."

"Yes, Mama, we shall be very quiet." Sarah eased her practised walk, for now she was just as graceful as any lady, nary a hint of a limp. She glanced back at the lovely new cottage that their father had built. The dwelling was a two-story thatched cottage, field stones stacked upon one another cast delicate brown shadows about the craggy blondish-brown surfaces. Lacy green vines grew up and around the white framed windows. Their old cottage was now two doors east, being used as the stables and carriage house.

Indeed, she was very proud to live in such a beautiful abode thinking often of his lordship Grayton, and dear Henry, whom she had not seen in well over five years. Her heart remained deeply troubled from the loss of her constant companion, she thought of Henry every day of life, but his lordship's sudden decision to remain in London was final, one dared not ask why.

This morning was a fair one with a few white clouds puffing about the skies. Sarah stood impatiently waiting for her aunt wondering what new book she would bring. She thought her Aunt Jane the prettiest lady she had ever seen, except, of course, her mother. They both looked very much the same, one exception being the colour of their hair. Her mother's was a bright red, Aunt Jane's was golden, almost white, and her eyes were silver blue and dreamy. She always spoke softly, and never had she seen her cross or out of spirits. Sarah loved her and oftentimes wondered if she should ever become as beautiful.

Jane poked her head out of her one-horse chaise, smiling and waving. "Hello, hello, Sarah!" William held the reins as the horse clopped along the narrow road.

Sarah always stood in that exact spot, to greet her aunt, that very spot on the road as it forked—one path to her home, one to the village. And when the chaise finally came close enough, she ran, never forgetting for an instant when she could not. And now to run alongside the horse was still a miraculous blessing. She often thought of Henry and what he would think if he saw her running. The wind dried her tears as they rolled down her cheeks, trying hard to keep up with the chaise; trying hard to put Henry in the back of her thoughts.

When they finally arrived at the cottage door, Jane stepped from the chaise with open arms and embraced her niece. "Oh, my Sarah, you run very well. Why, I believe the horse felt rather challenged when you raced alongside."

"I know, Aunt Jane, I know," trying to catch her breath. "I know. Now you must come in. Mama is waiting."

Jane and Anne hugged. "Come dearest," said Anne, "you must have a nice hot cup of tea."

"Very well, Sister."

Jane watched as Sarah moved casually and gracefully from the room making only a slight tap from her device as it touched the floor. "Anne, Sarah walks carefully as any cat, does she not? I do believe she'll be able to dance without a soul knowing that she is wearing the device."

Anne nodded. "She does. I do believe she has the will to accomplish anything she sets her mind to. I have never met a more pleasant and agreeable child in my life. Not because she is my own, mind. Sincerely, she is a beautiful girl. I only worry that she has never been exposed to outsiders. What would people think if they were to see her leg?"

Jane sighed. "I too, have thought about the same possibilities, Sister. Now that she is old enough to understand life, perhaps we should discuss the painful realities of rejection and ridicule. Would you trust so delicate a conversation to come from me? Sarah is a happy young woman. The happy ones, it seems, survive better than the rest."

"Indeed it is so." Anne paused for a few seconds, picked up the wrought iron poker and jabbed at the burning logs in the hearth. "Yes, I think such a conversation would best come from you."

"Very well, Anne, I shall be tender with my words."

"Oh, I have every confidence that you will. Tell me, have you heard lately from our dear Henry? The Misses Graytons have been very faithful in writing, but my heart is heavy, for I have not heard a word from him in many months, and then it is only a very brief note. However, the girls are delightfully witty, I should say, when they describe their London society. They are to steal away and visit us at month's end."

Jane giggled. "Indeed, Anne, upon my word, they plan very cleverly their visits from the ever watchful eye of their stodgy aunt, Lady Catherine."

"Lady Catherine must frown on her nieces visiting here. No doubt she is aware of us, but chooses to ignore it. For no wonder, his lordship pays her handsomely, once they leave the nest, she'll certainly feel the pinch."

Jane's face grew void of humour. Her ice blue eyes held a deep sadness. "And more often it seems that when they come and visit for more than a sennight, I worry that his lordship will be ill-tempered with me. But Anne, they truly love visiting with their sister Lady Margaret and me at the orphanage. You know Margaret is now twenty and quite the discerning woman, surely her father and Lady Catherine must understand that she owns her own mind."

Anne nodded in agreement. "But if Lady Margaret is removed from her care, her ladyship stands to lose a great sum; his lordship bestows a goodly amount for the care and protection of his daughters."

"Well, surely, Lady Catherine would not let money stand in the way of Lady Margaret's happiness."

"Perhaps."

"Victoria mentioned to me in her last letter that Lady Catherine was ill with cold and fever. It seems the whole of London is suffering from it. I have not heard more except through the villagers, that indeed a sickness is going about the city. The last freeze didn't kill the sickness completely, so take care in the orphanage that you and Margaret do not come ill."

"Not to worry, sister, Margaret is very capable with colds, for hardly a cough is heard anymore. And I do believe our little Lizzy is leaning toward her older sister's devotion to the mastery of medicine, she follows Margaret's every word."

"Ah, that is very good news, Jane. Elizabeth is so dear."

"Yes, I also hear a good deal from Victoria. She appears to be quite the discerning young lady about town. Her letters are full of news about London life—I fear she must find a very sentimental man to satisfy her whims, for she is such a romantic. She will not be satisfied with a stupid man. Indeed not, she is far too smart."

Jane laughed. "Aye, Anne, I should wonder at what part *we* played in their opinions."

Anne dropped her head in deep thought. "When dear Henry writes, he says he is near finishing his studies at Eton. He writes quite well, I dare say, and declares he is anxious to see us, but he has not been here in a very long time. I would hardly know him if he should come to our door. And to think, I would have wagered my soul that it would have been Henry that would remain close to us, but alas it has been his sisters."

"Aye," said Jane, trying to comfort Anne's disappointment, "it's just like a man to be so distant. Perhaps one day he will come pay a visit. He was such a dear, sweet boy as a child. Surely one does not outgrow such affections. He so loved Sarah, couldn't be near her for wanting to hold her hand—and you, why, it seemed he loved you as a mother."

Anne nodded sadly. "Indeed, now and again Sarah weeps for her dearest friend, as I do." She rose to stoke the fire again when someone tapped at the door.

"Good day, my dear Jane, so very good to see you," said Granny Whitmore as she closed the door behind her. "You look well enough."

"Oh, very well, indeed, Helen, and nice to see you as well."

The two exchanged pleasantries, kissing cheek to cheek.

"Sit here, Mother. I have arranged the chairs nearer the hearth. You shall be warm in no time. I will be only a moment with the tea."

Jane noticed Helen was growing old, stoop-shouldered, but her sweet disposition never seemed to change. "Helen, have you heard from your dear little friend, Lady Elizabeth, lately?"

"Oh, that you should mention my dear Elizabeth. I am so proud, mind, of teaching her French."

Jane pressed her hand, "And I have heard you even write in French."

"Oui, I show the villagers, and whoever else should see my post, that I *write* French as well as speak it. And now, Lizzy has taken quite a command of the language."

"You are a clever teacher, Granny Helen."

* * *

Two days passed quickly as they always did when Jane came to visit. And as they had but a few hours left before she was to return to Holybourne, Anne and Jane took a turn in the garden. It was a rainless spring morning; the grass had turned a rich blue-green, lush and abundant. The trees were not yet with foliage, and through their spindly, scratchy limbs hailed a brilliant blue sky. A few stark-white, billowy puffs of clouds tumbled slowly eastward. The air was clear and brisk, the type of chilly spring air that chills the lungs.

Pulling the hood atop her head, Anne nudged her sister with a shudder, "Take deep breaths, Jane. Remember, it cleanses the soul."

They held hands as they slowly made way through the unshaven damp grass.

"Anne, tell me, does his lordship's daughters ever mention the happiness of their father? I haven't heard that he chooses to remarry. I only ask because I still wonder about his well-being. I write to him often, he demands that of me. I must keep him informed of the orphanage and the children and of Margaret, of course, though she writes to him often.

"I never fail to mention and thank him for all the wonderful good works that continue to come from him. He is still most generous and kind. I realise that I am still very much beneath him in society, yet ..."

"Jane," said Anne taking her hand, "I understand. His lordship seems an easy enough man to love." There was a long silence as they continued walking along the garden path. "I know he was in love with you, Jane. I suppose a man in his position, with four unmarried daughters and a son, and such a man with eligible daughters in today's society cannot ignore their futures.

I know in my heart, if he had not such a family he would have married you. No, it is not fair. However, that is the lot in life in which we find ourselves. The very rich have their boundaries. It is very hard for me to comprehend loving someone so much and not being able to be near them. What a terrible price to pay, to sacrifice one's love for the happiness of one's children."

"Yes, Anne, I know ... I know very well. But, all the same, even understanding every bit of it is difficult." Picking a wild-flower, she brought it to her nose and breathed in its splendour. "He left Margaret with me to tend the children, as you well know, Anne, but, he has never come my way again these many years. I know I shouldn't complain, yet in his letters to me, I sense his affection still, for there is not one letter from him that he fails to seek my advice on something, often trivial matters. Or, if I am in need of anything, I must tell him immediately. And always, always, he makes sure to ask me something that I must reply post haste."

"No doubt he is still fearful of losing his self-control, Jane, over you. Why else would he not come to the orphanage in person? He must still love you deeply, that is the very reason." She pressed her arm. "I am very sure of it, dear."

"I think you are very right, Sister."

They soon wound their way back to the beginning of the path and returned to the cottage.

Anne giggled. "Oh, it seems we have spent too much time in the garden, and we now have a hungry family to feed. My husband smiles politely, but I can read that Sarah is not so inclined. I must warn you, again, about their hunger tantrums."

* * *

The very next morning, Sarah was up and about early on. She had been packed for days in happy anticipation of going back to the orphanage with her Aunt Jane for holiday. Soon after breakfast, she was waving goodbye to her family as William manoeuvred the chaise onto the well-worn path toward Holybourne.

Anne followed a little ways, stopping at the fork in the road. The mellow, soft white clouds, stretched long into the chilly morning air. She was shivering, for she forgot her wrap, but still she stood and watched Jane wave again and again with her little white handkerchief. They never stopped waving to each other until completely out of sight. It was an unspoken gesture the two shared since childhood.

Chapter 12 – King George Takes Ill in London

A deadly influenza spread throughout London, and it favoured no particular class distinction. Many of the elderly and the very young were dying at such a rate as to frighten the people into panic. The roads were lined with carriages and carts moving to the outer edges of the city in hopes of avoiding the fumes of burning beds and the stench from those decaying.

Most of the wealthy had already left the city for their country homes, and with them went their physicians. The only caretakers remaining in the city were the dedicated apothecaries, nursemaids, and midwives giving what aid they could.

The post carriers were reluctant to enter the city in fear of the sickness, so the mail delivery was sporadic, at best. The travellers that did enter London wore scarves about their noses, and in great haste, delivered goods in such scanty proportions that the poor had to make do with their own paltry supplies. Friends exchanged food as best they could, but they too were fearful to be cut off from the outside, and so they guarded their own supplies with their very lives. Unless a neighbour or friend was near death, they did not give much aid, for their fear was that they too could be stricken with the terrible sickness.

King George succumbed to the illness before he and the Queen had time to leave London. And now he was so ill with the fever and chills that he could not travel to the country. Queen Charlotte was beside herself with fear for his health.

While visiting with the King and Queen, Lady Catherine had been stricken as suddenly, and as violently. She was simply too ill to leave Norfolk-House. In laboured breathing, she sent word to the Queen that there was one person whom should cure the King (more importantly, herself).

The Queen, with a handkerchief to her nose, demanded, "Who is this physician then, pray tell, Lady Catherine, that *he* may make well my husband?"

"Your Majesty," she responded in a weak voice, "it is not a physician, but a young lady, my niece, Lord Grayton's daughter, Lady Margaret. She has the power to make me well again ... ah, make the King well again. I am sure of it."

"What is this I'm hearing? Upon my word Catherine, is the fever shrinking your brain? Lady Margaret, indeed," she scoffed, "preposterous."

"I assure you, ma'am, Lady Margaret is the very one. I am willing to lay my life into her hands. She has made me well many times over. She is a clever girl in all ways of medicine, I assure you."

The Queen's face puckered in doubt, but with few options left, she sighed, "Very well then, I suppose I must send for her immediately. I dare say my husband is not improving with those knuckleheads attending him. He is about drained with no blood left to let."

Her Majesty gave notice to her guards: "Locate Lady Margaret Grayton at the orphanage in Holybourne and bring her to the Palace at once."

There was much clamour and confusion in the Norfolk-House that morning. No one had seen such a flurry since the King, upon *suffering a spell*, ran naked in the thorny rose garden just a month past. Such a flourish of guards, coaches, and people scurrying here and there, with such expediency that within an hour's notice the Queen's men were on the Winchester-London Road to fetch Lady Margaret.

It was first light when the Queen's entourage rolled noisily into Holybourne; chickens squawked, dogs yelped, villagers peeked out their windows as the Queen's personal aide shouted to the passers-by, "Make way! Make way to the orphanage and be quick about it."

The village farmers, with their cows running helter-skelter, led the royal carriage to the orphanage's front steps. Standing back, the farmers were fearful as they pointed to the door. And there was such a violent pounding upon that door in the wee hours of the morning that Jane was fearful to open it.

Pounding on the door, the Royal Captain of the Guard shouted, "Open the door. Her Majesty Queen Charlotte summons Lady Margaret Grayton, and be quick about it."

Holding a candle, Jane slowly opened the door and peeked out, but a sudden rush of royally fashioned officials crowded past her. Pushing and shouting, they finally settled in the hallway, the flame on her candle wavered sideways and flickered to death.

A booming voice echoed throughout the orphanage, indeed, throughout the village. "Where is Lady Margaret, Lord Grayton's daughter?"

"I am here, sir." Margaret pulled her wrap up around her neck, her thick black hair, twisted into one long plait angled over her shoulder, "Pray tell, what is the matter that you nearly broke down our door? What message carries such an urgent arousal as this?"

"The King is very ill. Queen Charlotte summons you to London to cure him. Make haste, madam. Make haste. As well, Lady Catherine Bute is in residence at Norfolk-House, she is ill as well."

Margaret rubbed her eyes awake. "Indeed, sir, I shall dress immediately."

Sarah, cowering behind the door, held a candle up for her.

"I shall be but a moment, sir, to dress and gather my medicine." Margaret pulled Jane and Sarah along with her up the stairs.

The Queen's guards stood about the hallway, impatiently tapping their boots on the floor. The fashionably dressed courtiers sniffed around apparently finding the accommodations too meagre for their tastes and retreated to their carriages. They glared at the villagers who dared come too close. Even the horses snorted, stomped their feet, anxious to be away and back to their royal stables, royal rub-downs, and royal patronage.

All the cottages in the village were now aglow with candles. Curious little heads peeped from every window. The town's mingling busybodies gathered about the Queen's carriage, beyond wonder at the spectacle, afraid to question the stiff-backed, ill-tempered guards, but not to be unstrung, they remained.

Jane dressed immediately and sent Fanny to fetch Mrs Connor, the vicar's wife. "Bring her here now, even if she wears her sleeping gown."

Margaret sat at her toilette hurriedly brushing her hair. "Jane, you must come with me, I cannot tend to the King and Aunt Catherine without help."

"But of course." She turned to Sarah, "Dearest, you must remain here and help manage the children."

"Very well, Aunt, I shall."

Jane smiled at her compliant niece. "Mrs Connor and Fanny will watch over the orphanage, you must help them. You are very familiar with our ways here, and the children love you so. I hope to write to you every day." Jane sighed with a smile as she handed Sarah another note. "Give this to Mrs Connor. She will know what to do."

"Indeed, my sweetest girl," said Margaret, "please, will you write to my father of the illness in London. Tell him *not* to follow us. I will write to him very soon." With that, she leaned over and kissed Sarah goodbye, "I love you, child."

Sarah's little head was all a-spin. She bid them farewell with a wave. "I will do very well, Aunt. Go now and make well the King. Good-bye, Lady Margaret."

Within one-half hour of such a rude awakening, Jane and Margaret sat in the Queen's carriage, heading pell-mell on the Winchester-London Road for London. All the townspeople stood in the narrow lanes bewildered and in awe at such a spectacle. They waved good-bye, anxious for the troop to be clear, and well out of sight, before they should make way to the orphanage demanding an explanation.

"Are we dreaming, Jane?"

"Yes, Margaret, we are."

Chapter 13 – Henry Graduates from Eton

Lord Grayton and his daughters left London before the illness became so deadly and widespread. His lordship had long been absent from the great estate Rosewood Park, and he thought a short holiday there would do everyone much good. He anticipated with great pleasure his son's return from Eton and the happy prospect of entertaining his son's classmates.

Henry rode in the first carriage with his most particular friends, Miss Blanche Hamilton, and her sister, Ada, sitting opposite. Jonathan North sat next to him. The second carriage, following, held four classmates. Everyone seemed in good cheer anticipating a happy holiday at Rosewood Park. Besides, Henry's sisters, Lady Victoria and Lady Elizabeth, noted for their beauty, were to be there, thus making this holiday all the more enticing for the Eton men.

As the carriages neared the small village of Holybourne, Henry closed his eyes and reminisced about the old orphanage his father rebuilt years earlier. Living there still, he knew, was the beautiful Miss Jane Stewart, whom he once thought his father loved, but for coming to his senses, he was now associating with civilised, proper society. Indeed Henry understood exactly why his father so wisely disassociated himself from her kind.

He then thought of his sister, Margaret, still living at the orphanage. But he could not stop to pay a visit—surely an impossibility. How could one possibly explain that his sister chose to live with heathens? He couldn't even begin to understand her reasoning. *How could I explain?* he wondered in disgust. *Why she chooses to remain there in such deprivation?*—Well he simply chose not to.

Henry was mildly amused as he watched the lovely Lady Blanche sitting before him. She was silly, yes, but not quite as silly as her sister, Ada. They were handsome sisters, what with their blond hair curled about their bonnets, white, even teeth, gaiety and laughter at every turn. Oh, indeed, they turned heads.

Then an old familiar figure of a girl quietly entered his

thoughts, Sarah. The same girl that always came between him and every woman he took a fancy to. She came to him many nights in his dreams and always smiling ... a sensual smile. And upon awakening from such a smile in the deepest cleavage of night, his heated body was left tight and alone. He had to arise, splash water to his face. He knew not to try to sleep again for the shadows of her essence left him restless and brooding. He was unwilling to connect her smile to the stirring passion meandering deeply within his body. And now she was coming to him in his daydreams, and yet he continued to deny her. His body was very patient.

"Sir Henry," giggled Lady Blanche, "you are a dreamer, I see?"

Henry caught the prying edge to her voice. Annoyed, he turned his head slowly toward her. "What could have made you say such a thing, Lady Blanche?"

"You were miles away in thought, sir." She perceived his annoyance and softened her tone. "Though for being near Rosewood Park, I presume, lent you to such dreams?"

"We are nowhere near Rosewood Park." It was his tone and the sharp way in which he settled his shoulders that demanded silence. Clearly, Henry was not amused with her. He resented that she could even begin to guess at his most private dreams. *Dare she even come close to my thoughts.* He bristled and dismissed her with a sharp turn of his head. He leaned back looking out the window at the familiar rolling hills of Holybourne.

In his mind's eye, he followed the very path that led through the east pastures to the back of the orphanage. He envisioned the many halls and stairways that he and Sarah used to run through. They were children then, and it was there where he would hide in the cellar-way and frighten her as she hobbled to find him. He could always win at hide-and-seek. He never told her how he could hear the wooden *tap, tap* from her device. No, she never guessed how he always found her.

Ah, yes, then, her hair, he remembered how it glowed, being so flaxen. *I could find her anywhere—could pick her out in a meadow, in a crowd. Aye, that was my Sarah.* He exhaled a deep sigh and muttered her name aloud, "Sarah."

Then an inexplicable sensation gripped his body and moved from his mind slowly pouring over his shoulders, filling his chest, into each arm, down into each finger, moving into his back and into his legs until they would not move. And then that very fluidity flowing in his veins moved slowly to the centre of his being.

A fire of longing slowly found its way into his heart, squeezing it until he could not breathe.

He sat up abruptly bringing his hands to his face, wiping his brow and clearing his eyes. He took in a few deep breaths and tried to reason this feeling moving through his body and mind. He missed her far more than he dared to admit. And then the cold reality of having any affiliation with such a girl as Sarah Whitmore, a dirt-poor cripple, settled him.

Lady Blanche, in her high, silly tone, grated, "Sarah? Who is Sarah, sir?" She giggled, tapping his arm with her fan. "Come now, sir, you must tell us. We know of no one in our circle called *Sarah*."

The beautiful Lady Blanche suddenly became a bore. The absurdity of sharing his childhood memories with her was absurd. Indeed it was. She and her sister's shallow laughter brought to mind his idle days with his friends at Eton. How the destitute beggars were about the prestigious school, and how they would clamour about the carriages begging for a mere farthing. Oh, how the crippled hobbled about so bringing about the same shallow laughter as entertainment to him and his friends.

The Eton boys would fill their pockets with stones and then pretend to be throwing coins to them. Howling as the poor wretches waded into the freezing water to find but worthless rubble. He thought of the haunting despair in their eyes and shuddered at the vision. Deeply ashamed of himself for such conduct, ashamed and bored with this idle crowd he called his friends.

The very face of Anne Whitmore haunted him at every turn. And yet he could not explain to his friends who this *Sarah* was, this cripple, whose name he absent-mindedly uttered aloud just moments ago.

The young lad was in deep thought as the fast-moving carriages approached Holybourne. Up to the right, and not at a far distance, sat the orphanage on the hill. Many were about the grounds working the yards. It was a very handsome home after his father had it rebuilt, thought Henry, and he became angry when Lady Blanche pointed it out with ridicule.

She giggled. "Such entertainment, Henry, why just look there at the creatures staring at us. Cannot you see envy in their eyes? I should say they have not seen real beauty, distinction nor refinement their entire lives." She shook her head in disgust, pinching her nose, but unable to look away.

Her sister, Ada, laughed and sneered pointing at one woman in particular. "Just look, will you, at that fat old hag carrying a bucket of water. She's spilling more than she carries. Haha."

"I believe," said Henry quite warmly, "*that* woman is Mrs Connor, the vicar's wife. She gives of her personal time to help the orphans." His tone stifled the cruel chatter immediately.

"Humph," grunted Ada with an acid air of religiosity about her. "So be it, sir, but that still doesn't make her less disgusting."

Henry grew quite sullen.

Lady Blanche pressed her sister's hand, shaking her head. She whispered behind her fan, "Shush, he is in some sort of *mood* at the moment."

Suddenly, from the corner of his eye, Henry caught a strangely familiar figure of a girl running dangerously close to the carriage—very near his side window. At that very instant the coach jostled rudely to the left.

"Whoa there, whoa!" Frantic, the coachman shouted again as he pulled up tight and stopped.

Henry jumped out to see the trouble for himself. "Bless me, what is the matter?" He hurried to the horses and found them blowing hard, stomping their anxious hooves, foam spittle dripped profusely from their flailing mouths. Finding someone crouched low about the front carriage wheels, he stopped. "Who is that?" As he came closer, nearer the lead horse, there stood a young girl trying to soothe a crying child. He couldn't see her face for her large sun-bonnet hid it.

In grave redress, his coachman shouted curses at the girl. "You shouldn't have been so careless as to let the child run loose, it could have been trampled by the horses, killed by a run over!"

Henry shook his head, sneering. "Probably just another filthy rag and bone child—rat catchers, all of 'em. Shoo her away, now."

Looking up at the coachman, Sarah apologised, "Sir, I am very sorry, but I can only reason that this poor orphan should run to greet you thinking perhaps that her mother was in your carriage, coming back to fetch her, that is all. I am truly sorry that I couldn't move faster." She picked up the orphan, her wooden leg, in all her exertion to save the child, had shattered into splinters—a mess of dangling leather straps, buckles, and amidst her dangling foot, blood.

Henry turned back to rejoin his friends, but was mystified to hear them shouting and laughing. The girl who had just saved the small child was standing next to the carriage window; her torn frock exposed her crippled leg, now a broken wooden horror.

"What is that?" shrieked Lady Ada.

Both sisters huddled together staring out the window, one near atop the other, staring in disbelief at such a sight.

Jonathan North stuck his head out the window. "Freak, move away from the carriages." He spat at her and closed the window.

Holding the orphan securely on her good hip, Sarah turned her back to the stinging insults, tears streamed down her cheeks. Never before had anyone ever spoken to her in so evil a manner. She moved slowly toward the orphanage, limping.

Henry walked around the carriage, and when he caught sight of the girl's flaxen hair and limp, he knew, "It's her. It is Sarah." He glanced back at his friends, all watching her in disgust.

He stood mortified, too embarrassed to claim her as his old friend. His heart thumped a million times over. His dearest friend, Sarah, had grown up. He stooped down and picked up her torn and soiled bonnet. Wiping it clean with the cuff his frilly white sleeve, he overheard Lady Blanche remark at how he was blushing. He dabbed his forehead with the back of his hand and walked up the pathway following Sarah. Lingering in the air was the very same sweet rosewater fragrance that they both bathed in as children. His throat went dry; his face felt hot and flushed.

"Sarah," he called aloud.

She turned at the distantly familiar voice, and there to her utter amazement stood her long ago friend. "Henry!" she cried. Her eyes searched his face. The sweetest nostalgia moved through her body, loving him as she had always loved him. She thought him to have grown into a handsome young gentleman. Her face lit up with its old familiar smile, even as the tears were yet on her lovely face. "Henry," she smiled through her tears, "it has been so long. Why, I would have hardly known you were it not for your voice." She made a move to go to him, to touch him, hug him, but suddenly she sensed an ill feeling and stopped. Her beautiful smile slipped slowly from her face. She stared into his eyes wondering if this was really *the* Henry Grayton she once knew. "Henry, why do you remain silent?"

He did not speak, nor did he smile. He simply handed her her bonnet and stared into her lilac blue eyes for a very long time. Suddenly he turned and walked slowly back to his carriage. His friends remained silent. With a firm knock to the carriage ceiling, he directed the driver to move on. No one mentioned the affair, and no one said one word for the remainder of the ride to Rosewood Park.

Sarah stood on the porch and watched as Henry's carriage meandered up the narrow Winchester Road. Her heart, now in her throat, throbbed, exploding in tiny sobs. She felt a dark, black expanse envelope her body. Her good leg began to weaken and tremble.

Fanny took the fussing child from her arms. "What could the matter be, Sarah, that both of you are weeping?"

"Nothing matters, ma'am." Sarah wiped her eyes. "Please tend to Mary for me."

"Oh, indeed, Sarah." Fanny cradled the child. Something bad had happened, for she could not mistake the sorrow in Sarah's eyes. Glancing down, she noticed her ripped frock, her muddied bonnet, and her splintered device. "Oh, Sarah, dear, may I help you?"

"No, thank you, Fanny, I shall be fine." She remained staring out at the road, devastated.

"But, you're bleeding. Please ..."

"I'll be fine, Fanny, leave me." Her Aunt Jane could not have prepared her for the humiliation of being snubbed and laughed at. The words came pounding back—words that found their way into her heart with such a sombre and sober truth, 'Dearest niece, you know you were born special, and because of your deformity, God saw fit to bless you with a wonderful heart and a deeper understanding of those who do not have one thing special about them. You must guard your heart well, though, and not let it turn to stone. You will one day hear sharp tongues wag, receive silent glares, stinging words that will cut your soul into little pieces— but, hear me Sarah, you must turn your thoughts from such people, for they have not yet learned.'

Sarah desperately yearned for her mother, for she had never before felt such shame and embarrassment before. She looked up into the heavens wondering for the first time in her life why God chose to deform her leg. She found that it was not so easy to turn her thoughts away from unlearned people, her heart was broken raw, and at the age of fifteen, words of forgiveness did not come easy. But despite her despair, she tried to regain her dignity and self-worth as she stood in the cool evening air staring up into the heavens. "I know I must forgive them ... I know they have not yet learned."

Sarah had the depth of loving kindness to forgive, but there was something else deeply troubling her, a profound feeling of loss, a loss she instinctively knew her forgiveness could not alter. For hidden deep within her broken heart lay an insidious rumination of a cold truth that found its way into her innermost soul ... mingling its way into her prayers. It was a truth that came from the eyes of the one she so deeply loved and trusted as the dearest friend she had ever known. Indeed, Henry had stopped loving her somewhere in time, and she knew he would never come back.

Chapter 14 – The Holiday at Rosewood Park

It was but one day into their holiday at Rosewood Park, when Henry's Eton friends received word of the King's illness and the terrible sickness in London. Everyone decided they should leave for home to be attended by their own physicians, if need be.

They left, all of them, to the relief of Henry. He had thought only of the humiliation on Sarah's face as he left her standing at the orphanage. He was unable to speak to his father until now regarding his ill-mannered, ungentlemanly, conduct.

When the two were in the library, Henry was about to bring up the subject when there came a tremendous pounding at their entrance door. They both hastened into the vestibule just as Frederick, the footman, opened the door. There stood William Whitmore.

Grayton's face and manner softened immediately. "William, what is the meaning of such an arousal? Come in, man, come in!"

Henry stood behind his father, debating if he should embrace his old friend, William.

Muddy and out of breath from the ride from Alton, William managed a few words, "Sir, I have this post, urgent ... for you. Sarah wrote it from the orphanage just this morning. I saw your carriage pass just yesterday and knew you'd be here." After catching his breath, he turned and noticed Henry. "Henry, is that you?"

"Yes, sir." As he came closer, he was going to take his hand, but William reached out and hugged him as if he were still a little boy. Henry immediately felt at ease by this welcome show of affection. His inexcusable behaviour of silence these five years vanished. William's sincerity quite relieved him of his shameful conduct. There was still a very amiable affection for his old friend, and he eagerly hugged him in return.

"Sir," said Henry, as he smiled profusely, "how I have missed you and Anne! What has kept me from Alton, I cannot readily say, sir. Please forgive me that I have been negligent in visits and letters, sir. I am indeed ashamed."

"Nonsense, my boy, don't let that shame you one minute. Me and I understand, we understand, Henry, we do." He stood back. "Let me look good at you—such a tall, handsome lad, but no fooling Anne, she'll know you even being all growed up, I am sure of it."

Grayton stood back watching the two, smiling. Glancing down at the letter, he hemmed with sober breath. "Well, I must read your letter, William."

"Oh, oh, indeed, sir."

> *12 April 1788 - Holybourne Orphanage*
> *Dearest Papa and Mama,*
> *Aunt Jane and Lady Margaret were summoned by the Queen this very morning to London. The King is very ill, and Lady Catherine, Margaret's aunt, is there as well, and she is also ill. It was she who spoke of Margaret's way of healing the sick. She insisted that she come to attend the King! I cannot imagine such a thing as this happening to our family, but so it has. I am quite well, as the vicar's wife, Mrs Connor, is with me during the daylight, and Fanny, the cook, all the time. The children are doing very well ... they listen and are obedient. I only fear for Aunt Jane and Lady Margaret that they are in London where there is so much sickness. We have said our prayers this morning that our most gracious God in heaven protects them. I shall say no more Papa, I must go. It is now time for the children to play in the yard.*
> *My love, Sarah*
>
> *Oh, yes, Papa, Margaret wanted me to write to Lord Grayton and tell him not to come to London as their hands will be busy*

*enough. Please go to him and explain that she
will write to him soon.*

Just as his lordship dropped his hands in dismay, Victoria,
Mary, and Lizzy hurried into the vestibule.

"Papa," cried Victoria, "we heard William had come with so
urgent a message. Is something wrong?"

He handed the letter to Victoria, who read it aloud. Becoming more distressed, Victoria shook her head. "Papa, Maggy and
Jane are alone in London. I know they are with Aunt Catherine
and the Royal Family, but with the sickness there, what will happen to them?"

"Father, I shall go there immediately," offered Henry. "If
either should become ill, I will bring them home at once to be
attended by our own physician."

"No, no, my son, I shall go, they wouldn't listen to you. For
neither Margaret or Miss Stewart would ever complain. No, I
shall go and see for myself of their well-being."

Henry's shoulders straightened. "I shall go with you then,
sir," he said boldly.

With a smile, Grayton nodded. "Very well, then, Henry."

The Misses Graytons huddled around their father.

"We shall pray every minute you are away," said Lizzy, her
lower lip quivering.

"Now now, calm yourself daughter. We shall ride into London, and that is the whole of it. Nothing more should be made of
the matter." He turned to William. "William has graciously offered to have you stay with his family while we are gone."

Being very fond of the Whitmores, Lizzy nodded. "Very well,
Papa."

"Well then, your brother and I shall be on our way."

William hemmed, "Sir, I will be most honoured to come
along."

"Oh, no, my good man, you have done quite enough. I am
entrusting my daughters into your able hands—nothing is more
important."

William puffed up. "Indeed, sir, Anne and I will look after
them."

"We must now make haste." He glanced out the window.
"There is little light left, we must take advantage of what remains."

Chapter 15 – Norfolk-House, St James Square, London

It was the following morning at St. James Palace where Margaret and Jane had just taken a rare moment for tea together—it had been many days since they had the opportunity to speak with one another in peace. It was a fair morning in London. The spring birds were gathering in small coveys chirping in song as they picked through the crusty ice pack that still held strong to a few morsels of seeds and frozen insects.

Jane even ventured to slightly open a small window so that she could hear more clearly their sweet song. "Just listen to their chirps, Margaret. They offer such hope that all this dreadful illness shall pass away. The air even smells better already, I swear so," she said, smiling.

"Aah, Jane, you are right, indeed ... it does smell refreshing. Not the old familiar stench of burning. Indeed the breeze carries a chill, but not like yesterday with such blowing and howling and dark nasty clouds."

"Indeed, bringing night's darkness at such an early part of the day." She inhaled the refreshing air when she heard the King stirring. "I shall see what he is about, Jane."

"Aye, Margaret, I'll look in on Lady Catherine and then we shall finish our tea."

Margaret hurried to His Majesty. She found he was trying to climb from his bed. "Sir, what are you trying to do?"

"Eh?" Surprised that someone should dare challenge him, he responded in a hoarse voice, "I think I am able now to walk about on my own. I can safely say, besides this nasty cough, I am well on my way to good health. Where is my wife?" He dangled his heavy-set legs aside the bed. "Where is my wife?"

"I will bring her, sir—after I help you walk a little about the room." She led him a few paces, steadying him as he took a few steps.

He studied her face. "Who are you, then?"

"Sir, I am Lady Margaret, Lord Grayton's eldest daughter. Perhaps you did not recognise me, and for that I cannot find fault. I have long been absent from Court."

Glancing at her, he grunted, "So you have. Well, your aunt shares the same illness as mine."

"Yes, sir, Aunt Catherine is just down the hall. She is being tended by my dear friend, Miss Jane Stewart. Aunt is also feeling very much better when last I saw her this morning."

"That is good news."

"Sir, I think you have walked enough." She escorted him back to the bed.

As he bent over ready to climb in, he wrinkled his nose. "What is that I smell, pray tell, what is it?" He eyed the window Margaret left slightly ajar. "An open window in my room?" he frowned.

"Yes, sir, the illness about London is now slight. There is not one ill wind to be found. Nay, sir, but only freshness and good health blow about your room."

"Aye, but at this moment my arse is cold."

"Oh, goodness me, Your Majesty, yes, of course, it would be." Hurrying to close the window, she giggled. Returning, she helped him to bed just as Queen Charlotte bustled into the chamber.

Upon seeing her husband with colour in his cheeks, she became giddy with happiness. "My dear husband, that you are all wellness, I cannot believe my eyes." She took his hand and kissed it over and over.

He gestured toward Margaret. "Charlotte, is this young *fairy* responsible for curing me of such a dreadful sickness?"

"Oh, yes, dear husband, the very one."

"Then give her Ireland, Scotland, and the London Bridge."

"Aye, my beloved King, and is there anything else I should do for you before I rub your cold, achy feet?"

"Aye, rub my cold, achy arse."

Margaret burst out laughing. Then the King and Queen joined her in hilarious uproar echoing throughout the palace.

Such laughter startled Lady Catherine awake as she lay but a few doors away. "Miss Stewart, I cannot imagine such glee in the house, what with the King being so ill and all."

Jane fiddled nervously with her handkerchief. "Oh, I am sure something or the other tickled His Majesty."

There came a tap to Lady Catherine's bedchamber, and Margaret entered. Finding her aunt sitting up, Margaret smiled.

"Well, well, Aunt Catherine, pretty as any picture of good health on this beautiful spring morning, I see."

"Indeed, Margaret, Jane and I heard such a rattle of noise. Imagine laughter when His Majesty is trying to regain his health."

Giggling, Margaret assured her, "Have no worries, Aunt. His Majesty has recovered. He is feeling much better."

"Well, it is only because of you, Margaret, and you, Miss Stewart. I dare say I have misjudged you, niece. Indeed I have, and I must confess, even from the beginning regarding your dedication to becoming a physician." She sighed heavily, "If not for you both, I wouldn't be alive this beautiful spring morning, nor would the King be laughing."

"Thank you, Aunt." She took her hand to her heart. "Thank you for understanding." She turned to Jane. "Well, Miss Stewart and I have much yet to do this morning. Please excuse us. We shall be back shortly, Aunt, with your breakfast tray."

Lady Catherine held her handkerchief to her face. "Oh, very well, then, if you must leave me, go."

Before Margaret and Jane closed the door behind them she was snoring.

"I do believe she shall survive," whispered Jane with a wink.

They both gave weary sighs as they made their way back to their study and rang for tea.

"I should think my aunt shall nap for a good while. Let us take a few minutes to finish our tea." Margaret shook her head, "And, I must write to father and inform him that all is well and that everyone is mending quite nicely. We have, after all, been gone a fortnight at least, Jane."

"Aye, without even a minute to write, but I shall write Sarah this very instant and inform her that we should be home within the week. As well, I must write to Anne to set her nerves in good order."

Chapter 16 – Jane's Letter to the Whitmores

Since the illness in London was finally easing, the post deliveries resumed their normal schedule and Jane's letter to the Whitmores' arrived at Alton within two days. Anne and William were relieved to hear from Jane and that His Majesty was well. London was finally coming back to life, and soon they would be coming home.

"That is very good, then," said Victoria as she and her sisters gathered around Anne as she read aloud Jane's letter. "Oh, certainly a letter from Father and Henry should be waiting for us at Rosewood Park. Oh, happy days, Papa and Henry shall be back soon, as well."

The sisters were giggling and dancing around the study when a sudden knock at the door interrupted their frolic.

Oliver, the footman from Rosewood Park, stood in the doorway. "Miss Mary, a post has come. I thought you should be aware that it is addressed to Sir John Grayton, from Lady Margaret Grayton, Norfolk-House, London—I am concerned."

"A letter from Margaret to her father?" said William aloud, "but his lordship was supposed to be there by now, with them. Why, he and Henry left a fortnight ago for London."

Mary nervously ripped open the letter and read it aloud, "April 20? That cannot be.

20 April 1788 - Norfolk-House
Dearest Papa,
Thank you for not coming to London,
dearest. Stay where you are, safe and sound.
We have heard that there are bands of ma-
rauders about the highways looting and preying
on the helpless that were fleeing London from

*the illness. To be sure, Miss Stewart and I
are doing very well, it seems -- a little ragged
perhaps, but well. The King is in good spirits,
and so is Aunt Catherine. They are too weak
yet to move about with ease, but they shall live,
I assure you, Sir. I beg your pardon for not
writing sooner, but it has been near impossible to
find a letter carrier, nor the time to write. Slowly, now we see more and more of our neighbours
coming back into town. Jane and I will be
home within the week, well, as soon as the King
dismisses us.*

Your affectionate daughter, Margaret"

Mary stood with the letter in her hand, frowning. She didn't know right off what to make of the matter, but William did. He knew something had befallen Lord Grayton and Henry, but he knew well enough not to frighten the Misses Graytons.

"Why, do not be alarmed," he said in a soothing tone. "I wager Lady Margaret's letter was sent ahead just as your father made his way into London, and their paths crossed. It happens frequently, I dare say. I imagine him to be sitting by their hearth this very minute."

Anne smiled in agreement, but she knew the Misses Graytons were nervous. "But of course, William," Anne assured them, "do we not think the worst of things right off, when in truth it is a simple thing all along? Come now, let us have some tea."

William nodded to the footman. "Oliver, I have a plan that will ease the hearts and minds of us all."

Anne nodded. "Oh, indeed, husband, please share it with us."

"Oliver and I shall ride into London, to St. James Palace. Oh, I can see their surprised faces this very moment—your father, Master Henry, Lady Margaret and Jane. We shall then return home instantly and report back to ease your troubled minds."

"Oh, dear," said Anne, "that sounds the best of plans."

"Indeed," smiled the sisters.

Lizzy kissed William's cheek. "Thank you, sir. Do be very careful, won't you?"

William and Oliver left to make their plans. While at Rosewood Park, preparing the best horses for their ride into London, Oliver frowned. "Mr Whitmore, I do hope his lordship is safe and that the roads are free of riffraff."

William patted his vest pocket, "No worries, Oliver. I have a fine pistol with me."

"Aye, sir, that is good."

* * *

Anne Whitmore remained cheerful for the Grayton sisters. "See there, my dears," you must have no worries. William has set off for London and will be back very soon with good news. You shall see, within a few days I am sure we shall once again hear the fuss and clatter of many carriages filled with happy smiling faces at our door."

When finding a little time alone in the quiet early morning hours, Anne wrote to Sarah.

My dearest Sarah,
Thank you for your letter. I do not mean to frighten you, but no one has heard from his lordship or Henry -- they left for London the very day we received your letter regarding Lady Margaret and Jane going to London. It was within minutes of reading your letter that, Oliver, Grayton's footman, came with a letter from Margaret, but by the date posted, his lordship and Henry should have been in London by days. Margaret did not mention them, only saying she and Jane would soon be home ... hopefully within the week. She was relieved her father had not come. London is only a matter of hours by carriage, as you know, but Grayton and Henry rode horseback, which should have made their arrival even sooner.
And so now your father has also gone to London in search of them! The Misses Gray-tons are with me now and, of course, are anxious

to hear from their father. They will remain with
me until he returns, hopefully very soon. We are,
of course, anxious for everyone's well being. Your
father has not let on to any alarm, but he is
worried. Pray as I have taught you,
    Your loving mother

Chapter 17 – Left for Dead

As Sarah walked with the children about the orphanage grounds, she noticed a courier riding toward them at high speed. To her utter amazement, he stopped at the gate. The children converged upon him.

"A letter for Miss Sarah Whitmore," shouted the young man.

"I am Miss Sarah."

Breathlessly he slid from his mount and handed the letter to her.

She searched her pocket. "Oh, I am sorry, sir, I do not have a penny for your trouble."

He tipped his hat. "Been paid already, miss, I knowed this an orphan's home, no matter." His face coloured as he watched the lovely young girl anxiously rip open the letter. The orphans crowded around her, clutching her skirt.

Sarah smiled. "Oh, it is a letter from my mother." She read it aloud, but kept the worry in her heart from her ward's ears. "Well, it looks as if Lady Margaret and Jane will be home soon."

The children hopped about the grass, twirling and doing cartwheels, clapping at such news.

The courier jumped atop his horse, smiled at Sarah, and galloped away, occasionally glancing back at her until he was finally a speck of brown, swishing horsetail.

"Now then," she smiled down at the worried orphans, "are you satisfied, children?" She folded the letter and stuck it in her apron pocket. "As Miss Jane has written in her last letter that as soon as our good King says she and Lady Margaret may go, then she shall be coming home, I assure you. I am just as anxious as you to see them, after all, Jane is my aunt, and Lady Margaret my very particular friend. Now, do you understand my sweet little cherubs?"

* * *

It was the oldest orphan boy, Charles, who first spotted the bodies lying along the Winchester Road, half-clothed. He heard a moan and thought it was his dog, but the moans came again, louder. Rushing back to the orphanage, he found Sarah sitting on the porch trying to repair her broken device. "Miss Sarah, come quick. Make haste!"

She knew by the tone of his voice that something was very wrong. Flesh bumps ran up her spine. Standing, she steadied herself on the porch railing. "What is the matter, Charles?"

"There be bodies layin' in the road, miss." He pointed. "Come quick!"

The children stopped their rollicking and hurried toward Charles. Some ran to Sarah, clinging to her side. "Bodies? Then come away this instant," she demanded. "Go no closer."

Trembling and breathless, he nodded. "Yes, ma'am?" Hurrying to her side, his face grew paler.

"Charles you must run to the smithy, Mr Hamm, and bring him."

At the news, Hamm dropped his irons, and for having just readied the wagon for his wife, took it from her. He shouted for his helper, Connor, to join him. Soon the smithy, Charles and Connor were making their way along the Winchester Road at great speed.

Approaching the bodies, Charles pointed. "There, sir, you see them?"

Hamm reined in the horses as Conner jumped from the wagon. Cautiously he approached the bodies. "Well, they's ain't blue and stinkin' yet." He touched one. "By God, them is alive."

Hamm stood over Connor's shoulder staring down at the men. "Good God, Conner, for sure they are alive."

They gently lifted each man into the wagon.

"They's alive, but by a hair," said Hamm.

"Where'd we take 'em? I ain't room at my place," said Conner.

Familiar with not being wanted, Charles knew exactly where to take them. "To the orphanage, Miss Sarah will know what to do with them."

"Aye, boy, that we will."

The smithy tried to hurry best he could, yet be easy with the wagon. Finally, they reached the orphanage. Charles jumped out and bolted through the door shouting, "Miss Sarah, Miss Sarah."

She hurried into the vestibule. "What is it, Charles?" She found Hamm and Conner carrying the strangers into the orphanage.

"Miss Sarah, them men I found is alive. I told the smithy to bring 'em here, cause there ain't no room nowhere," said Charles. "Them are hurt, miss."

"Where'd ya want us to lay 'em, ma'am?" grunted Hamm.

She glanced around. "Oh, let me think." She turned to Charles. "We have no spare beds, so we'll put one in my bed and the other in Miss Jane's room. Hurry now, Charles, show them the way. Fanny and I shall bring blankets and water. Oh, and one more thing, Charles, you must find the apothecary and bring him here at once."

Sarah settled the worried and anxious orphans, explaining what was happening. "Be patient until we cleanse the men. We need to make them comfortable until the apothecary comes." She glanced up at the cook. "Fanny, I will cleanse the man in my bed, if you would bathe the one in Miss Jane's room."

Fanny nodded. "Aye, Sarah, that I will."

* * *

Sarah pulled up a chair next to the injured man in her room and removed his tattered shirt. There were gouges and cuts, mud and filth in his eyes, ears, and mouth. When she washed his hands, she found them to be a gentleman's hands, though his nails were torn and bloody. She glanced at his mud-caked feet. "La, they have even stolen your boots, sir."

One trouser leg had been ripped up to his knee. She removed clumps of dried grass held fast to his skin as she cleansed him. Had it not been for the man's soft hands, she would have thought he a mere vagabond left along the highway. "Obviously sir, you have been robbed by the many thieves picking their way through the London gentry fleeing from the influenza."

Now gently wiping the caked mud from his face, she was careful not to let the dirty water seep into his eyes. The more she cleansed, the more familiar his face. "You are an older gentleman, perhaps the age of my father, sir." When she combed the dried mud from his hair, she noticed colour had come to his cheeks. She gently lay his head on the clean, white pillow and stood. Now standing at a distance, she gasped in astonishment, "No, it cannot be, but ... it is Lord Grayton."

His lordship's eyelids quivered slightly as he moaned. "Aye, it is him," she whispered. "I wonder who is in *my* bed then? Do they know each other, surely they must."

Sarah laid a quilt over his lordship and hurried to her room. Fanny was gently washing the other man's face, a young man's face. "God in heaven, it's Henry."

Fanny, startled at her words, sat back in amazement. "Sarah, you know this lad then?"

"Aye, I do. And the man in Aunt Jane's bed is our master, Lord Grayton, Rosewood Park. And here lies his son, Henry." She took his wrist and felt his warm pulse. "Upon my word, where is that apothecary?" she fretted. "He should have been here by now."

Fanny nodded. "We need to get some broth into 'em both."

They hurried into the kitchen. Sarah scooped two bowlfuls. "I'll feed Henry, Fanny. Hurrying up the stairs, she called back, "Oh, and I must write to Mother of our find."

Chapter 18 – William Arrives at Norfolk-House, London

William was shown into the Royal chamber for receiving commoners. It was within a short time the inner door was opened by a well-attired footman and Margaret. She hurried out. "William, what brings you?"

"Lady Margaret, perhaps I have come in haste. Are your father and Henry here?"

"What do you mean, William? I sent word for him *not* to come to London—there was so much illness about."

"Lady Margaret, I am sorry, but he and your brother were quite concerned over your well-being and left Rosewood Park to find you, and that was well over a fortnight ago."

"A fortnight? Why, no, they have not come here." She sat down, mumbling, "A fortnight?"

Jane came into the room. "William, what is the matter?"

He kissed her cheek. "Sister, it seems that Lord Grayton and Henry are missing. They left for London a fortnight ago to join you here. They were concerned about your well-being … "

"Oh, dear me, no." She touched her throat as if trying to take in a breath. Turning pale, she looked into his eyes. "How can this be? His lordship coming here? And Henry is missing, too? Oh my, but this cannot be." She took Margaret's hand. "Oh, dear, surely nothing could have happened to them, let us pray nothing has happened to them."

"But they have been gone a fortnight." Jane looked at William. "What is to be done?"

Suddenly the doors opened, and Queen Charlotte entered.

"Your Majesty," said William, overwhelmed at standing less than two feet from her, in the same room, taking in the same air. He was mortified for not knowing what he was supposed to do, bow? Curtsy? Do nothing at all?

"What is so worrisome that you both cry?" asked the Queen. Turning she noticed William. "Pray tell, man, what is the trouble you bring?"

Margaret hemmed, "Your Majesty, my father and my brother Henry travelled to London a fortnight ago—to find us and to make sure we were not ill. No one has seen them since," she cried into her hanky. "I fear, we all fear, robbers, thieves, and the like, have brought them harm, why else the absence?"

The Queen looked at William.

Margaret hemmed, "Ma'am, this gentleman is Miss Jane Stewart's brother-in-law, Mr William Whitmore. He has just arrived with the sad news."

The Queen's manner softened. "Dear me, Lady Margaret, I am shocked to hear it. John and dear Henry? Why, I named Henry myself, so I did. How should harm come to them?" She seemed as dumb-struck as everyone else and sat wearily in a chair.

William remained staring at the Queen, in awe. Never in his entire life had he been in such a lavish house as this, nor standing so close to royalty. The Queen was visibly upset, and he supposed not many commoners had ever witnessed such emotion. *Why, I'm close enough to touch her tears.*

As he stood there feeling helpless, wondering what he should be doing, the Queen instructed her lady-in-waiting to bring the Captain of the Guards to her, immediately. Within a minute there was a clamour just outside the door, and then came a slight knock. Her lady-in-waiting entered. "Ma'am, your Captain of the Guards is come."

Captain Smith entered and bowed. "Your Majesty, at your service, ma'am."

"Captain, this gentleman whom you see standing there," she gestured to William, "has brought distressing news that Lord Grayton and his son, Henry, have met with ill dealings somewhere along the King's Highway from Rosewood Park. They left a fortnight ago and have not been seen since. You are to find them and bring them to me." Her voice dropped as she opened her fan and whispered behind it, "Alive or otherwise, but they are to be found."

"Ma'am," Smith bowed, "I will leave this very minute. You may be assured, Your Majesty," he said with much aplomb, "that I will not rest until I find them." That said the highly decorated officer left in a flourish of feathers and flapping red coats.

The Queen soothed Margaret and Jane in a motherly tone, "There, there, my dear ladies, I have sent my Captain. He shall find them soon enough. Such a puzzle that both have disappeared, but not to worry, my dears, we shall find them."

"Thank you, ma'am, thank you," said Margaret, dabbing her eyes.

"Indeed, Your Majesty, thank you," said Jane, becoming more upset by the minute.

"Miss Stewart, you have no colour to your cheeks. I dare say you must take leave and lie down perhaps."

"Yes, ma'am, I do not feel well, thank you."

Margaret watched as Jane bowed her way from the room. "Ma'am, Miss Stewart has been very much in love with my father these many years. Circumstances and her station in life have not permitted them to marry. You see, she and her sister are twins and were abandoned at the Holybourne Orphanage when they were babies. Miss Stewart stayed on and has become headmistress there. Her sister, Anne, left the orphanage and married Mr Whitmore." She nodded to William as he stood quietly. "He stands just there."

The Queen gestured for him to sit. "Please, Mr Whitmore, do sit down."

Margaret continued, "The Whitmores are a dear family. He and his wife, Anne, in fact, schooled Henry in his elementary years. Perhaps you remember my father speaking of them?"

A faint memory stirred her recollection. "Oh, indeed." She paused. "Well then, Lady Margaret, tell me, what is this business with your father regarding Miss Stewart?"

"Father is very much in love with her, but considering her questionable birth and station in life, he has not kindled the relationship. Lady Catherine has also encouraged Father to shun such a woman, fearful such a bad proposal would damage the prospects of his daughters. Father is not a happy man, Your Majesty, and I cannot succeed it seems in making him reconsider his options and marrying her—he thinks of everyone but himself."

"Lady Catherine objected? Ha, she seems to have forgotten her own history. One would think she would be more understanding."

"Ma'am, Miss Stewart is my particular friend. She has been like a sister to me. She loves Father unconditionally, and as you have just witnessed, she is worried sick over him and Henry."

The Queen affectionately patted Margaret's hand. "Indeed."

"Ma'am, I beg pardon to take leave. William and I must post a letter to his wife, and I must write to my sisters."

"Certainly you may, Lady Margaret." When she turned to leave, she faced William. "Mr Whitmore, you have been very quiet."

He bowed feeling deeply ashamed of his appearance. *She must think me a savage farmer indeed.*

"It was very good of you to come, though under sad circumstances."

"Your Highness, it was nothing at all." He spoke with his head bowed, not knowing if he was allowed to look her in the eye.

"Mr Whitmore," she said kindly, "I would wish it that you stay here at Norfolk-House until it pleases you to leave. Lady Margaret will show you to my study. I shall have someone attend you both with writing paper. As well, you may make your plans regarding Lord Grayton and Henry."

"Thank you, ma'am." William bowed.

The Queen turned to Margaret. "The King is in very good spirits, weak but no longer ill. Lady Catherine has recovered quite nicely as well. I shall inform her of his lordship and Henry's disappearance, and I shall inform His Majesty of your family's predicament. Go then, go into my study, it is a smaller and warmer situation there."

"Thank you, ma'am, you have been most thoughtful and kind." Margaret curtsied.

William nodded, ignorant of proper protocol. The Queen stood for a few seconds then smiled at the humble man. She finally realised how bewildered he must be and simply left the room.

William smiled at Margaret. "The Queen is really very pretty, Lady Margaret." He fumbled with his words. "Do forgive me … I dare say, I embarrassed you."

"Rest assured, William, you will never embarrass me. Come, I shall show you to the library. We must discuss what we shall do about Papa and Henry."

"What is there for us to do, Lady Margaret? Nothing, but sit here and fret. Her Majesty is sending her guards. I think it best we go home."

She shrugged. "Perhaps you are right. Very well, then, William, I am most certain His Majesty will release us. He is now well recovered from his illness. Yes, I believe we would all be more comfortable at home. I shall be only a moment, then. I must find Jane. We cannot make plans without her."

Chapter 19 – All the Queen's Men

There was a hurried mass of the Queen's personal guards as they, in great haste, mounted their silky, raven-black horses to go in search of his lordship and Henry. All twenty-five of the Red Coats moved through the narrow London streets. The marketers, young children, and shoppers scurried along the narrow cobblestoned roadways slipping into crevices, doorways and stoops.

"Oh, my dear husband," said the Queen as she rushed into his chamber. "Oh, dear me, such news I have for you."

He set down his sherry. "Such news, indeed, I can hardly wait to hear it."

"Come then to the window and see my Guards. I have sent them to find Grayton and Henry."

"What? Lord Grayton? His son, Henry?"

"Well, it seems they came to see how you were coming along, and what do you suppose came of it?" she said all a breath.

Glancing out the window at the guards, he frowned. "What came of it, Charlotte?"

"Lord Grayton and Henry left Rosewood Park a fortnight ago, but no one has seen them since. Is that not dreadful news?"

He moved away from the window and sat heavy in his chair. "Why, I am shocked."

"My guards will find them, sir."

"In one piece, I pray."

"Oh, indeed, in one piece ... it must come about, for such a great man and his son cannot simply vanish. Grayton is loved by so many, particularly that lovely maiden Miss Stewart—the one attending Lady Catherine and you, sir."

"Grayton loved? What do you mean, Charlotte?'

"Apparently he has been in love with Miss Stewart for years. Lady Margaret has informed me that Miss Stewart is very much in love with him, sir. And, of course, at hearing such dreadful news, she has gone to her room in shock."

"Where did she come from, Charlotte and why haven't I been told of the affair?"

"Well, no doubt Grayton realises she is well beneath him in station. Lady Margaret told me she and her sister are twins. They were left at the Holybourne Orphanage well over twenty and five years ago. Miss Stewart chose to remain at the orphanage and is now headmistress there. Grayton found this Whitmore family— you remember, dear, the ones who schooled Henry?"

The King shook his head. "Charlotte, you are speaking all aflutter, again." He frowned. "Slow your speech ..."

"Oh, well, I beg pardon, my love. Ah, where was I? Well through that connection somehow Miss Stewart fell in love with our Grayton and he apparently, with her," she sighed.

The King shook his head. "Why are you sighing?"

"Oh, my love, it is only ... that John has fallen in love with the wrong woman, I am afraid."

"I am at a loss to your meaning."

"Must I?" She fanned her face. "After all she *was* placed in an orphanage, sir and, therefore, cannot marry our Grayton, I am sorry to say."

He nodded, rubbing his chin. "Indeed, marry an orphan, impossible. Think of the complications ... and then what if their family reappeared and claimed the twins as their rightful daughters."

"Oh, I quite agree, sir. Grayton has wisely removed himself from her in order for his daughters to become well married—he has four you know."

"Four? Dear me he will be far too old to find a proper wife by the time they are all married off. No man should ever be deprived of ..."

The Queen blushed. "Oh, I made sure of that ... that you would never have deprived yourself, sir."

He sighed deeply. "And to think, he could have his pick of any woman he wanted, all eligible women ... pity his choice."

"The heart loves despite reason, sir."

"And so it does." He shook his head. "Grayton is my staunchest ally, my greatest friend ..."

"Oh, indeed, sir, and he has been your most loyal supporter these many years."

"Charlotte, together we must simply find a way to help Grayton."

"You mean a way that he may marry Miss Stewart, sir? Why that's an impossibility – even for a King."

Taking a forlorn glance out the window, he sighed. "Well, if they don't soon find Grayton and Henry, it will all be for nought."

Chapter 20 – Margaret and Jane Leave the Palace

The King and Queen were in their private quarters with Lady Margaret and Jane Stewart.

"Your Majesty, we have found it necessary to leave Norfolk-House and return home. We need to tend to the business of locating my beloved father and brother, if we may be excused, sir?" said Margaret.

The King assured her all the guards were out and about the highway from Rosewood Park to London, throughout the countryside. He and the Queen were quite sorry over the entire affair. It was apparent their sincerity was genuine, for rarely did their Majesties grant a morning visit and forgo breakfast with their children.

Jane was in such awe of their human side. Indeed, their informality in dress and manner around her and Margaret. But of course, fifteen children born to the couple was surely the reason. They were not in the least ill-mannered, rude, or demanding, and appeared very devoted to each other.

An odd feeling struck Jane as she thought back while tending the ailing King. Betimes he would call her Sophie. 'Sir, my name is Jane, Miss Jane Stewart. 'So it is,' the King would answer, all the while watching her with furrowed brow, as if pondering something over and over again.

The servants told Jane not to mind the King, 'For many days he confuses names easily, and many days he does not even remember the Queen, even as she lies next to him.'

Interrupting her thoughts, the King walked to the hearth lifting his tails to warm at the fire. "Very well, Lady Margaret and Miss Stewart, you may go. You will take the royal carriage. The palace guards shall transport you to Holybourne in safe order. But you will come back betimes and sit with us, I command it."

Margaret and Jane stood. "Indeed, sir," said Margaret, "we will be most honoured to come back. We are only too happy to have helped in your recovery to good health, sir."

Jane nodded. "We pray Your Majesties live long and happy lives."

The two bowed their way from the room and joined William, who was waiting with the footman, Oliver. Suddenly the door flew open, and they were surrounded by Red Coats and the King's personal guards.

Jane nodded to William. "We have been ordered by His Majesty to take his royal equipage." She climbed into the carriage. "Come now, we have much to do before the sun sets."

Once situated, William spoke in a whisper, "Sister, you must tell me, is the King as odd as everyone says?"

"No, William, he is not."

Oliver glanced about the rich interior. "Aye, I'll never ride in this again." He glanced out the window at the people as they stared back at him. Smiling, he waved.

Jane ran her hand over the plush red velvet seats. "I'm even afraid to place my feet on the footstools." In awe, she touched the highly polished mahogany handclasps, ledgers, and trim. "Just feel the sleek windowsills, marbled burl, so warm it is to the touch."

The royal window shade was embossed in gold lettering and filigree with the King's royal crest. The door handles were ornately twisted black iron. There was even an elegant *smell* to its interior, thought Jane. "Lilacs, yes, the fragrance of wild lilacs, the very same fragrance that lingered long after Her Majesty quitted the room. Nay, I shall never forget this moment in time as long as I live."

"Lavender is Her Majesty's favourite," said Margaret, "and mine, as well."

Finally, as the morning sun intensified into the noon's hottest peak, the royal entourage stopped at an inn halfway to Holybourne to rest the horses and comfort its passengers.

Crowds of idle passers-by hurried out to witness the important personage that should come from the royal carriage. Could it be the King? William was first to step down, then Oliver. The crowd was perplexed, indeed disappointed at their simple manner and dress. And when the two ladies stepped down, they were not attired in fine clothes, nor bejewelled, nor with fine plumed hats. They were all in wonder at such a sight—just who were these *plain people*?

They gleaned nothing important, however, from these royal travellers. But, nonetheless, they would be the topic of conversation at the Bentley Inn for hundreds of years to come—and to be sure, some historian will take note that someone of royal patronage stepped foot there.

It was but two additional hours when the royal carriage finally rumbled into Holybourne and went straight away to the orphanage. With all the excitement and clamour of the horses, and with the King's Royal Guards clomping and making important noises, all the villagers gathered about, excited at the spectacle.

A small committee of orphans stood in awe as they welcomed the weary travellers. A few dared come past the gate, mesmerised by the King's red-coated Royal Guardsmen atop their magnificent black stallions.

Jane, now out of the carriage and satisfied that no immediate trouble was at the house, kissed the happy children. She asked them to find Fanny and inform her that Mr Whitmore would spend the night.

Margaret welcomed the children, hugging them in turn. She explained how exhausted she was, promising to see them all in the morning. Margaret and Jane and William and Oliver stood on the front porch of the orphanage and watched as the King's royal carriage ceremoniously circled the town, surrounded by the Royal Guards, and then made their way along the Winchester Road back to London.

Jane and Margaret, being near exhaustion, went straight away to their respective rooms, anxious to cleanse the dust from their faces, clothes, and hair.

"I shall join you for tea, later, Margaret. Perhaps we shall then find where Sarah and Fanny have run off to."

"I should say. I rather think William would have found Sarah by now." She affectionately kissed Jane on the cheek. "For tea then, dear, later."

Jane entered her dimly lit chamber and found a warm, delightful fire, thinking only how wasteful to have one going in an empty room. As she walked to her privacy screen to change, she stopped momentarily and lit a candle from the fire. She held it carefully pushing the soft tallow end into the pitted brass cup and then carefully set it on her night table. As she reached for a fresh towel, she was again amazed at seeing her water bowl full and fresh, with clean linen lying by its side, neatly folded.

"How should they know I am home?"

But she was simply too tired to think upon the matter one second more and began to undress. She lit the small candle that sat beneath her jar of rose oil, taking in its sensual fragrance. She gazed at her appearance in her small hand-mirror and smiled, "I do not look so very old ... under candlelight."

The journey from London was a long one, and it felt good to remove her tight, road dusty frock, camisole, and stockings. Tossing each article in a neat pile at her feet, she stood naked, and sat to cleanse herself. Then the most savoured ritual of her bath ... she luxuriated in the warmth of the heated rose oil that she rubbed on her weary, achy body, marvelling at the silky appearance of her skin. Afterward, she sprinkled the ashes-of-roses powder on her clean under-things, tied her robe lightly to her body, and began brushing her long flaxen hair, twisting it by turns and then finally letting it fall to her waist.

When she turned to leave, she noticed a figure of someone lying on her bed. In the darkness, she could not make out more, for her bed curtains hid the face. Her hand shook as she held up the candle, her voice trembled, "Who are you? And what are you doing here?" She inched her way closer. "Is that you, Mr More?" She moved even closer, the sense of it all coming clearer. "Indeed, the poor confused old man must have come into my room by mistake. Poor old soul, he is near deaf."

She was calming herself over the pitiful old man's mistake. She felt her face burn with embarrassment had he awakened and found her bathing. When she gently pulled back the curtain, she gasped. "Good God, Grayton?"

Hot wax dripped onto her hand. "Ouch," she pulled back the curtain farther, "Sir?" He didn't move at her words, his eyelids flickered for a second and then went still. She perused his face, touching his forehead, it was warm, not feverish warm, and she was relieved. "What is the matter here?" She could feel her heart beating wildly in her throat.

She sat in the chair by the bed, placing the candle on the night table. She put her fingers to his neck feeling a strong and steady beat. Laying her head on his chest, she felt the easy rise and fall from his breathing. His skin was soft and warm. Examining him closer, she didn't find a mark to give reason for his deep slumber. But wait, as she turned his head, there it was—a dark bruise near his right ear.

She had not seen him in years, and as she caressed his soft, warm hands she studied each long and tapered finger, fancying a quill in one of them, writing to her; perhaps love letters. Yet she was quite aware of the impossibility of their union. She whispered his name again and again and then put her lips on his, he did not move. Bringing his hand to her eyes, she wiped away her tears. "He lies in my bed? What strange circumstances bring him to me this way?"

* * *

Margaret learned of her father's head injury from Fanny—the dilemma of his deep sleep. He was not recovering soon enough. After she found Henry healing satisfactorily, she hurried to her father's side. She quietly entered Jane's room, and there she found her sitting by her father's side clutching his hand to her teary face.

"Jane, dear," said Margaret, "he sleeps deeply, for such a blow to his head, apparently, near killed him."

"I thought as much, Margaret. Who would have bludgeoned him so severely, I am in such wonder? Who should want to do such a thing to such a kind man?"

Margaret set her candle near Jane's adding a bit more light. She watched the peaceful and handsome face of her father. "Oh, Papa, Papa, please hear me," she whimpered. She tenderly kissed his cheek and felt the warm prickle of his beard touch her lips and caught the mildest fragrance of rose oil on his skin. "I love you, Papa."

There was silence in the room for a few minutes. Jane finally opened her eyes and stood, laying his hand gently to his side. She touched Margaret on the shoulder. "Come, Margaret, let us go."

Margaret nodded, bent down and kissed her father's forehead. Both left the room, walking side-by-side down the stairs, in silence. They reached the breakfast room where Jane found tea and biscuits; she poured for them both.

"Sarah is presently with William," said Margaret softly. "She will join us soon. Fanny says Sarah has been like an angel. Bless her, and she has taken very good care of Father. She has been too embarrassed, though, to look in on Henry until he falls asleep. Fanny said something *occurred* between the two most recently, but Sarah chooses not to divulge the details, only that she somehow displeased Henry exceedingly. And she is quite convinced she would repulse him even more if she made her presence known to him."

Jane looked up in surprised wonder, "Sarah? But she is an angel, Margaret. What discord could she bring to anyone?"

"I dare say, on that score, Margaret, she would not confide in me. I had only a few minutes alone with her, and she wishes not to speak of it. I have always known her to idolise Henry. Well, you know exactly, she has loved him since childhood. He, in turn, loved her, I am convinced of that. For my life, I cannot reason the matter that Sarah, of all people, should carry the notion that she would repulse him, could repulse anyone for that matter."

Chapter 21 – Sarah Mends her Dress

When Sarah heard from Fanny that Henry was finally awake and alert and that he would soon be up and about the house, she made haste in a few last minute seams to her dress. And there, in her quiet and thoughtful repose, sitting nearby her candle and delightful fire, she worked her needle. With idle mind, she searched again for a meaning to Henry's disgust with her, recalling the day she saved the orphan from being run over by his carriage, and again feeling deeply ashamed for embarrassing him in front of his friends. After seeing the look of disgust on Henry's face, she knew she could not let him find her nursing him to health, especially in the very same dress.

Her mind was not settled, and again, she questioned his behaviour, "But why should he be angry with me?" She reasoned only that she was so much beneath his notice now that he was *of age*. And as she pushed the needle into the cloth a vision worked its way into her thoughts, "Of course," she sighed with heavy heart, "I am a painful, nasty reminder of his childhood affiliation with me."

She was aware of class distinctions and her low society. Her mother and father explained the classes and stations to her long ago—she knew her place. Just like Aunt Jane knew hers, but she never stopped loving her sweet and happy boyhood friend, Henry. She missed the deep and close friendship they once shared as little children. And she wanted that feeling in her heart again. She wanted to continue to love him, the grown-up Henry. But alas, she reckoned, he was past all that, "he was a man now." And she sighed feeling a terrible melancholy fill her heart.

"Ouch!" The sudden prick and rush of blood to her finger brought her back to her work, her frock, and her ugly deformed device looming large, slivered, and crooked on the footstool. She cried as a small droplet of blood spilt onto the only unspoiled part of her dress. Tears dripped freely onto her fingers. "Oh, I am so clumsy." Suddenly she felt a hand touch her shoulder.

"Sarah, why are you crying?"

She looked up—startled for she had not heard anyone come into the room.

"There now, let me help you." Noticing blood on her finger, Henry bent down. "Here, let me wrap it, Sarah." He reached over and pulled away the patch material she had laid over her leg and gasped, "Good God, Sarah, your leg!"

He was shocked at how mangled it had become; her little foot had been bleeding. When he looked into her eyes he felt her deep anguish—Sarah, no longer the shy child, had grown up into a beautiful young woman. But now her face was distorted, humiliation in her eyes, tears streamed down her cheeks, dripping onto her hands, onto the sewing needle now frozen in space.

A deep sense of shame enveloped his body. He wrapped his arms around her. "Oh, God, Sarah, I am sorry." All the years of his childhood amassed before his eyes and throughout each scene Sarah was always by his side, holding his hand, laughing, giggling, never crying; never like this. *What have I done?*

He went to his knees and put his arms around her leg, around her foot and kissed it. Weeping quietly, he pleaded, "Sarah, please Sarah, forgive me." He held her little foot, "Somehow I shall repair this, rest assured, Sarah."

He then began slowly and gently, reverently, removing the leather straps, ties, and buckles. With his soft and gentle hands, he soothed her swollen foot.

She fondly ran her fingers through his soft, chestnut brown hair. "Of course I forgive you, Henry."

He brought his head up, smiling. "Sarah ..." Sitting up, he took her hands kissing them ... kissing her arms, her neck, he wanted to kiss her cheeks, her eyes. He took in her sweet breath as he kissed her lips over and over.

She felt his tears and tasted the sweetness of his mouth, she felt the soft whimper in his throat, and he came closer until his heart touched hers. And still she wanted him closer, *but how could such a thing exist?*

He moved away gently, trying to calm his breathing. "Sarah, I will never leave you again, never. I am going to marry you, Sarah. Then I will take you to a place so near heaven that you will then understand how two people can become one."

"But Henry," she murmured softly, "my heart will break if you do not put your lips back on mine." Her eyes searched his until she recovered enough to realise where she was, and blushed at his nearness. Looking around hoping the children had not seen them together, she took his hand, amazed at how quickly his lips could blind her to every other live thing around her. "I love you, Henry."

Chapter 22 – Sarah and Henry Join the Others

Early the following morning after Jane and Margaret looked in on his lordship they decided to take a quiet respite in the morning room. The orphanage was beginning to stir; old Mr More was about his task of stoking the kitchen fires as Fanny prepared the breakfast.

Margaret poured tea for herself and Jane. "Two sugars this morning?"

Jane nodded. "Yes, please." Cradling the cup and saucer, she sighed heavily. "Your father is breathing easier it seems this morning, Margaret. The physician will be returning this noon." Blowing at the vapours, she shook her head. "I suppose there is nothing more to be done."

"Dear me, Jane, you mustn't lose hope. Father is a very strong man."

"If only he would awaken."

A slight pause came over them when Sarah and Henry entered.

Margaret set down her cup and saucer. "Why, Henry, where is your walking stick?"

Sarah removed it from beneath her arm. "Henry forced *me* to take it, Margaret."

"That's right, she needs it more than I," said Henry bracing himself on a chair.

"Is there something wrong with your device, niece?" said Jane

With the aid of Henry's walking stick, Sarah slowly made way to a chair and sat clumsily. "Do not worry, Aunt Jane, Henry has made my foot comfortable, I can wait."

"Wait? Wait for what?" said Margaret.

Sarah lifted her skirt.

Jane and Margaret gasped.

"No, you cannot wait. We must work on it now," said Margaret. "I'll find some wood and reuse the old buckles, but in the future, young lady, you mustn't deny yourself help."

"But there were more important things to think upon, than myself."

Henry lay his hand on her shoulder. "You are just as important as anyone, Sarah. You must stop putting yourself last."

"But with all this fuss over me, we are not preparing for the arrival of Mary, Victoria, and Lizzy, for they are coming today."

"Oh, they are not in the least concerned about comfort at such at time. And for now, we must look after your foot," said Henry.

"How did you manage to break it so thoroughly, Sarah?" said Jane.

"She dashed to grab a child from falling beneath my carriage," said Henry. "She slipped and fell." He glanced down in shame. "I am deeply ashamed to say I didn't go to her, to comfort her, to help her then. I grieved over my ungentlemanly behaviour the entire night, and the following morning I was going to apologise. I was just beginning to explain to Father my intentions when William came to our door, we then immediately had to prepare to leave for London. I convinced Father to stop at the orphanage on our way so that I could speak to Sarah.

"We were not far from Holybourne, as we could see the candlelight flickering from the orphanage's windows. It was then that highway robbers broke in front of us and demanded our clothes, boots, and gold. When Father challenged them everything went black. I remember nothing after that until waking here.

"Fanny told me where they found us." He shuddered. "It's something I will be very happy to soon forget." He stood. "Well, I must go now and sit with Father."

Sarah took his hand. "Indeed, we shall both go."

Chapter 23 – Lordship's Family Arrives at the Orphanage

It was mid-day at the orphanage. Just as Margaret finished fixing Sarah's device, she heard a carriage, barking dogs, and the scurry of the children. Peeking out the window, she found a handsome carriage pulled by four very fine greys stopping in front. "It is our carriage, Sarah. My sisters are come."

The formality of *welcomes* was done away with. The Misses Graytons were pale, tired, and very anxious to see their father and brother. Anne was last to step from the carriage, William helped her down.

Sarah, now able to walk without a cane, helped Henry to the door. "You may lean on me, sir," she offered, "for now I am ..."

"In perfect order, Sarah," he said, squeezing her hand. "And forever more."

His sisters rushed up to him hugging and crying.

"Calm yourselves, sisters, I am safe. I shall be fine. As you can see, I am alive and healing."

Lizzy hugged him. "Oh, Henry, you gave us such a fright."

"So you did, brother, such a scare, indeed," said Mary and Victoria gibbering together, their white lace handkerchiefs fluttering about.

"I will take you to Father ..." He suddenly noticed Anne approaching. Hugging her warmly, he smiled. "Oh, Anne, how I have missed you."

"Dearest Henry, I have missed you as well." She looked him up and down. "We have all been worrying so about you."

Dark circles worn about his eyes; Mary and Victoria stood close to him, nervously fussing over him.

"How is Papa?" cried Lizzy. "I want to see Papa, Henry."

"Father is resting," he gestured, "just upstairs."

Anne knew immediately by Henry's looks and manner that he had not changed, though now quite the handsome gentleman. She instantly forgave his prolonged absence, a mother's redeeming quality. He appeared very much the dear sweet boy he had always been.

Henry turned, steadied himself on his cane, and winced. "I am still very sore, so forgive me for moving slow. But come, we shall look in on Father."

Sarah welcomed the sisters with subdued embraces and teary-eyed smiles. She whispered to Henry, "Mama, Papa and I shall visit with your father later."

"Sisters," said Henry in a low tone, "this way." He slowly climbed the stairs using Lizzy as a crutch.

"Father and I were robbed along the King's Highway very near here. I cannot remember much about the affair other than Father was furious with the rascals. He was very brave and put up a gallant fight, but there were too many of them. They stripped us of our clothes, boots and gold, leaving us for dead." He winced. "Sarah and Charles, he's an orphan here, found us. Without them, we would have perished."

Gently opening the bedchamber door, Henry and his sisters entered the room and found a very nice fire in the hearth. The air snug and comfortable; the aroma of spiced apples and rosewater filled the air. Jane dozed in a chair by his side, holding his hand. To their surprise, lying atop their father's pillow, curled in a ball, slept a cat.

Lizzy wiped her eyes, shaking her head with a giggle. "Papa detests cats ..."

Mary and Victoria walked softly to the foot of his bed. Henry put his hand on Jane's shoulder, her eyes sprung open.

"Oh, dear me, I must have fallen asleep." Jane gently returned Grayton's hand to his chest. Rubbing her eyes awake, she soon regained her senses and nodded solemnly to the family. She turned to straighten his lordship's covers and sighed. "Oh, dear me, that rascal cat will not stay away." She whispered apologetically, "No matter how many times I shoo it away, he finds his way back." She shrugged. "He insists upon lying on your father's pillow. I am sorry for it." She held a weak smile, her expression strained.

Lizzy took her hand. "Thank you, Miss Stewart, for caring for Papa so lovingly."

As the cat lifted his head at the annoyance, Lizzy peered down into his face, but he simply yawned, perused the audience, and then curled back up into his fuzzy tail and nodded off. Lizzy shook her head in amused wonder. "I understand the ways of cats, Miss Stewart, they are like me ... they hate to be bossed."

Lizzy's humour broke the heartsick strain. Her sisters tried to subdue their nervous laughs and then resumed staring at their father's expressionless face; the only movement being the flicker of warm orange flames dancing sprightly on his lordship's stiff, motionless, mummy-like form.

Victoria took his hand and patted it gently. "Papa, dearest, I love you, please wake up, Papa." She pleaded many times over, but he remained motionless.

Mary brought his other hand to her lips, weeping.

Lizzy kissed his forehead and then gently caressed the big cat's furry head. It purred loudly at her kindness, but still it did not move off the pillow.

"Excuse me, but I am still very weary." Henry inched his way into a chair and slumped into it.

Jane quietly quitted the room, leaving the grieving family to their father. She found Margaret in the hallway. "Your family is with his lordship at the moment."

"Oh, indeed, I watched them arrive. I found Anne and William in the parlour. Sarah is with them."

"We shall await tea for you there, then." With that Jane moved down the hall checking first on all the children making sure they were doing their lessons. When she entered the parlour, Anne hurried to her side. "Come, dear Sister, sit here. You look very tired. I am so sorry to hear the news."

"Oh, indeed," she said with a weary sigh. "It has been a long few days, Anne. I am exhausted with worry."

Sarah took a chair directly across from her. "Indeed, Aunt Jane, you must soon lie down and rest. You've not left his lordship's side for a minute."

She nodded. "Perhaps tomorrow morning will be one of fairer skies."

Chapter 24 – Norfolk House, St James Square, London

Queen Charlotte awoke from a dream that set her in a happy mood, a very happy one indeed. As she lay staring up at the familiar damask ceiling cloth that hung heavily over the royal, ornately carved, mahogany four-poster bed, she smiled. "Manfred, but of course," she mumbled, trying to arise from the many pillows scattered about her head. "Indeed, the resurrection of a long forgotten cousin shall solve the puzzle."

Pulling the Queen's bed curtains aside, her maid curtsied. "Your Majesty, your cloth and water await you."

"Bring my physician," said the Queen, smiling.

The maid frowned. *Her Majesty never smiles from her morning bed, why then the physician? Could she be with child, again?* "Yes, ma'am, I shall bring him. Am I to tell him what ails you?"

"No, I had a very happy dream that is all. Summon Lady Catherine to me for tea after my breakfast meal. Then later, I shall walk with the Recorder of Antiquities. I wish to walk the Hall Gallery where the King's ancestors hang. Prepare him, for I shall need the proper ancestral books for my reference."

"Yes, ma'am, as you wish."

Everything went quite well that morning. The Queen loved yellow, and that was precisely the colour gown that was brought to her. Her hair was combed, and without one knot pulling her tender scalp. Oh, indeed, she was pleased. Yes, this morning was a lovely one, her mood remained exceptional.

"Is my husband awake?" she inquired.

"Yes, ma'am, but His Majesty has left the palace. He is gone shooting birds in Odiham and Horsdon Common, two days full."

"Very well then, bring my physician, now."

It was within in minutes when the physician was escorted into her chamber. With deep concern, he bowed. But when he looked directly at the Queen, all concern evaporated. The sun was shining full upon her face, and in her yellow gown, she glistened in good health. Her face radiated. "Your Majesty is not ill … you shine like the very sun."

"Oh, most poetic of you, Physician, most poetic," she moved away from the window. "Wilfred, I wish that you should look in on the Earl of Grayton. He is, at present, situated in the village orphanage at Holybourne."

"Lord Grayton … at an orphanage, ma'am?"

"Indeed, His Majesty's most particular friend was beaten quite severely a few days ago. Imagine, accosted by robbers along the King's Highway. I heard he is still in a deep slumber. One fears death may be near. You are to see him and bring your summation of his health to me, at once."

"Indeed, ma'am. I shall leave this very minute."

"One more thing, Wilfred, surely you remember Manfred, my husband's Cousin Manfred, Southsussex, born but two years after the King." She snorted with a half-laugh. "A cloth headed dimwit if there ever was one. Ah, yes, he lived but twenty and six years."

Scratching his head, he mumbled, "Ah … no, Your Majesty, I cannot recall such a birth."

"Well, Wilfred, there *was* a birth, I assure you. He married a very ambitious woman who died an unfortunate death – birthing twins."

"How dreadful, ma'am."

"Indeed it was."

Not wanting to cast doubt on the Queen's memory, he hemmed. "Well now, ma'am, I do seem to recall some sort of birth event." He lied. "Manfred, you say, ma'am?"

The Queen looked pleased. "I knew after a moment's recollection you should remember, Wilfred. I am certain it was *your* father who assisted in Manfred's birth—yes, I am quite certain it was he. Well, no matter, Wilfred, you must go now to Holybourne. Do all that is necessary in securing Grayton's well being. However, consult first with his family and with a *particular* acquaintance of mine who is Headmistress there, Miss Jane Stewart."

She then moved back into the sunshine and gazed down into the courtyard listening as her physician left the bedchamber. Shortly thereafter the footsteps of her chambermaid were heard following the opening of the door.

"Ma'am, Lady Catherine awaits."

The Queen entered her private study where a snappy fire

burned in the hearth, a full silver tea service sat elegantly nearby. Iced sweet cakes and fruit tarts were situated on a thrice-tiered white-china platter.

"Sit, Lady Catherine, sit," said the Queen. She noted her ladyship wore a pale green gown with a darker green muff and hat trimmed with Russian sable. She always looked rather pale in green, but the Queen was in a very happy mood and chose not to mention it. Reaching for a sweet cake, she chuckled, "Lady Catherine, you must join me."

"Indeed, Your Majesty," she nodded with a smile, "after all, I must obey my Queen."

Giggling, they helped themselves to more sweet cakes.

"So, ma'am, I must know why you have summoned me." Catherine bit into her cake. Rarely did the Queen summon her but for personal, urgent matters and usually for quelling an ill mood of the King's. Catherine had the uncanny ability to soothe him with her tales of intrigue, usually gossip and made-up tales, but the Queen didn't mind. She only wanted her husband returned to his humour and good senses, and she always paid Catherine quite handsomely.

"Lady Catherine, you of course remember Manfred, Viscount Southsussex, His Majesty's cousin?"

"Cousin?"

"*Distant* Cousin, Lady Catherine."

Her ladyship's brow furrowed. Panic seised the *know-it-all* of Royal history, scandal, gossip—well, she faintly recollected him. She squinted up at the chandelier, "Yes, I think I remember there was once such scandal. "Ah ..."

Speaking with her mouth full, the Queen dabbed her lips. "Really now, Lady Catherine, you must recall his wife, Agnes. Together, you and I thought her altogether a brazen vulgar bore."

Catherine stopped chewing, her brows still furrowed in thought. "Agnes?"

"Indeed," said the Queen. "She had two daughters, twin births." Biting into another sweet cake, crumbs spurted from her lips. "Oh, but the scandal, such a scandal, I shall never forget it."

"Oh, yes, Your Majesty, I quite remember it now. Oh, but it was so soon covered up. Why so cleverly covered up I myself could hardly recall it." She swallowed hard trying to keep the wrinkles of doubt from spreading across her face. Thinking of the possible bauble that would await her recollection, she sighed with a smile. *Oh, I must remember such a birth.*

"Yes, and the infants and she were never seen again. Manfred died and the whole of it forgotten."

"And what do you make of it now, ma'am?"

The Queen smiled. "You shall soon see, Lady Catherine." With that, the Queen held out a silver tray. Sitting atop was a lovely diamond-studded brooch. "Good day, Lady Catherine.

* * *

Remaining in her sitting room, the Queen heard someone at the door. "Come."

"Ma'am, the Royal Recorder of Antiquities has come."

The Queen stood with a smile. "Very well, bring him."

In came a tall, skinny, insignificant-looking little fellow. He bowed. "Your Majesty."

"You are Recorder of Antiquities?" she said. "Let me see your little book there, and what is your name?"

The recorder was so nervous at meeting the Queen in a private tête-à-tête he could only mumble his name. As he handed her his *sacred book*, he dropped it. Mortified beyond belief, he bent down with red-faced, flustered disarray and retrieved it, apologising profusely for his clumsiness.

The Queen was satisfied with her choice of finding such a fellow. "Your name again?"

"Peter Pepper, ma'am." He bowed so low his breeches parted ways.

"Mr Pepper, you are an expert, they tell me." She eyed his little book. "All royal heritage, births deaths, everything has been entered herein?" She eyed him with doubt. "Even where the portraits hang? All in this little book of yours ... in ink?"

"Oh, yes, Your Majesty."

"You will walk with me and point out particular portraits along the Hallway of Ancestors, Mr Pepper."

He sniffed the air holding out his sacred little book. "Every oil painting hanging in the palace is listed in this book, ma'am. Where they hang, how long they have been there, their lineage and rank of importance. The higher the rank, the closer they hang in proximity to your residence. But, of course, ma'am, you know that already."

"All written there in that small book?" She eyed the red velvet, cloth-covered little gem.

Pepper opened the book, cleared his throat, and with arched brow, confidently showed at random a page, assuring her, "As you can see, ma'am, my hand is small and neat, precise and," he gloated, "without one ink smudge, written therein, everything in perfect order."

The Queen glanced at the open page. "Very good."

Pepper was overwhelmed that Her Majesty favoured him with smiles. His head was in a flurry of glee. *Wait until I tell my wife, my children ... I shall finally be esteemed for my merits these many years of cataloguing the oil portraits of the royal families. Ooh, la la* and his buttocks began to twitch.

The Queen smiled as she moved down the hall, the silly little twit at her side.

The Recorder of Antiquities was springing along with a happy step indeed, and near the end of the Great Hall, she stopped suddenly. Backing up a few steps, she stood before the oil of Manfred Curl, Eighth Earl of Southsussex.

"Recorder," she said with a question dangling in her voice, "how can this be? I have passed his picture a thousand times. How should my husband's cousin Manfred Curl be called an Earl? How should such a mistake come about?"

Pepper's throat went dry, he squeaked, "A mistake, ma'am? Why, that *is* Manfred, the Eighth Earl of Southsussex. There cannot be a mistake," he said staring at the brass plate secured to the ornate, gold-filigreed frame. There etched: *Manfred Curl Eighth Earl of Southsussex.*

The Queen looked aghast. "Oh, but there is a mistake, for that is definitely the King's cousin, though distant perhaps. Oh, if the King should notice his beloved cousin placed at such a distance from his door, he would not be pleased. *We* are fortunate in finding the error. You will consult your Ancestral book, Mr Pepper, and correct the oil immediately. Hang it in its rightful place."

The Queen wrote him a brief note:

The Viscount Southsussex, Manfred Curl was born 1730 and died 1755, he had two daughters, twins: Sophie and Juliet, 1755, their mother was the infamous Agnes Moore who died in labour; the girls survived. Use this to verify that your book is correct.
H.R.H, Queen Charlotte

Chapter 25 – Queen's Physician Returns with Sad News

Wilfred, the Queen's personal physician, had just returned from the Holybourne Orphanage and was escorted into Her Majesty's personal sitting room.

Bowing deeply, he hemmed, "Your Majesty, I am sorry to say I have been to see Lord Grayton, and I find little health in him. He has lain in slumber much too long—far past the time when one should awaken from such a blow to the head. I fear he has not long to live ... his pulse is very weak, very weak indeed." He shook his head sadly.

"I had my fears, Wilfred. I will go to see him, to bid my farewell. Say nothing to His Majesty. I do not want his mood altered. I shall inform him myself, later."

"Yes, ma'am."

The Queen gazed out over the rooftops at a bit of rolling green meadow in the far distance. It was raining again and the dark churning clouds added to her sadness. She bowed, shaking her head in sorrow. "He was such a dear friend."

* * *

The Queen's entourage to Holybourne was limited to a few Guards only. She chose not to use the Royal carriage, but the plain one. She wanted to make haste, see his lordship and return. In miraculous time, she changed from her day gown into a plain brown travelling ensemble, not fretting about her hair—only covering it with a lace scarf.

"Make haste now," she commanded, "I must return before seven this very evening."

* * *

William Whitmore arrived at the orphanage just as the Queen was being escorted into the parlour by a few orphans.

"Well, I am pleased to see you again, William," said the Queen. "I am here to see his lordship ... show me the way to his room."

"Your Majesty," he bowed deeply. "We are honoured."

As they passed through the refectory, they bumped into Fanny. Looking startled as the Queen approached, she dropped her freshly baked biscuits. "Oh, I, I beg pardon, Your Majesty ..."

Giggling, the children hurriedly picked the biscuits up. Eyeing the newest visitor with question, they put them back into Fanny's apron.

The Queen's nose twitched as she eyed the delightful smelling biscuits. "May I?"

"Oh, indeed, Your Majesty." Curtsying in clumsy fashion, Fanny almost spilt them again. "Oops, oh, beg pardon, ma'am ..."

The Queen plucked one from Fanny's apron and noticed the children staring. One little girl, about four, began to whimper. "Who are you?" she asked.

Patting her head, the Queen smiled. "Well now, child, you find sadness in my coming?"

"Have you come to take us?"

"Oh, my no – why, I have fifteen children of my own."

"You have an orphanage then, ma'am?" said Charles looking puzzled at the magnificent women standing so elegantly before him.

She smiled. "I have an entire realm of orphanages, young man." Turning to William, she nodded with a sad smile. "Well, I must be about my business. Show me where his lordship rests." She smiled a good-bye to the children.

"This way, Your Majesty."

Entering the room, William nodded to the Misses Graytons. When they saw the Queen, they curtsied deeply and respectfully moved away. Jane stood in awe. Henry took her arm and led her and his sisters from the room.

The Queen placed her hand on his lordship's shoulder. Teary-eyed, she removed her brooch with King George's likeness painted on it. Pinning it to his sleeping gown, she took his hand. "Rest, my dear friend, for the King and I shall pray for you—for your arousal, to hear your happy tones, your kindness, and your sweet ways when you are about my husband and me again. Good-bye."

The Queen found her way into the hall where she found

Henry. She could see how puffy his eyes and how red his nose. "Come, my dear Henry, let us go now and join your family. Nothing more can be done here. It will be your father's will to open his eyes. I have seen as many miracles in my travels. Hold hope in your heart, my boy."

Chapter 26 – A Premonition Grips Jane

The house was stone silent the rest of the day, long after the Queen departed and long into that evening. It seems Her Majesty's presence was one of finality for everyone. Jane had a premonition, a feeling deep within her soul, and if it should come to pass this night, she wanted to be with him. She shared this feeling with no one.

The darkest hour came as she held his hand and felt his pulse race, then slow, then race again. Suddenly the old grey-striped cat's head came up off the pillow. It cocked its head and peered directly into Grayton's face, its whiskers touching his nose.

Jane watched in sleepy wonder at the cat. Just when she was about to shoo the annoying feline away, his lordship's head moved slightly. She took his hand and felt his pulse. It was strong and vigorous. Her own heart pounded.

"My love, my love, wake up, my love." Tears dripped freely onto his gown. "Wake up, my lord, oh, please, wake up." Exhausted, she laid her head on his chest and wept.

The ominous, dark grey, early morning fog slowly curled its way around every single structure, tree, and bush alike in the village. The orphanage looked strangely singular, sitting back from the road, surrounded by moss green hedgerows with only a lonely black wrought-iron gate to its entrance.

One could hear the steady drip, drip, drip onto the rain-soaked boardwalk beneath the gate's ornate metal turnstiles. The thick, murky grey dawn was slow to wake the exhausted household. This day's morning would arrive late, owing to the heavy mist that coated the dust-laden windowpanes.

Jane awoke to a very cold room; the fire had gone out. The big grey cat was curled around her arm. She felt the soft beat of its little heart, its deep purring. There was calmness about the room, and calmness about her. It was still quite early, greyness filled the chamber.

Her one hand lay on Grayton's chest. He was breathing still, slow, and deep. Jane touched the soft underside of his neck, just

near his ear. A soft, strong beat. She moved her lips to that softness and kissed him, again weeping and praying. Then she gently
moved her arm from the grey cat, leaving it to its slumber.

"I shall rekindle the fire," she whispered aloud rubbing her
arms briskly. "Oh, but I am chilled through and through." Glancing down, she shook her head. "No wonder, my shawl lays at my
feet."

She wore her softest white muslin sleeping gown, sheer and
full. Her long, yellow-white hair hung loose and long about her
shoulders. Before moving to the hearth, she took Grayton's hand
to her lips and whispered her morning prayers.

Opening his eyes, he found her in prayer ... her head bowed,
the dawn's first light softly tracing her lovely silhouette. Her sil-
ver-white hair cast about her shoulders made her appear to be
an angel. Her hands were warm and tender. He could smell the
slightest fragrance of rosewater about her lovely presence. It was
quiet in the room. "You are an angel, have I died and gone to
heaven, Jane?"

Startled, she pulled back her hand. "My lord, you awaken?"

Glancing around at the unfamiliar room, he slowly shook
his head. "Well, it matters little where I am, Jane, as long as you
are with me."

She kissed his hands, his face; his face again and again. Realizing she was half-dressed, she wrapped her shawl around herself, smoothing her hair, blushing. "I have prayed night and day
for you to wake, sir."

He smiled tenderly at her adoring gestures.

"Oh, I must go now, sir, and wake the household. All our
families are here."

With that, she hurried from his side, but instantly returned
and took again the liberty of kissing his hand, his cheek and his
lips. Her loud, happy cries aroused everyone. Soon the entire
house, in their sleeping gowns and caps, were at his lordship's
side, laughing and talking all at once.

* * *

In the weeks following, Margaret, his constant *physician*,
tended to his every need. Jane's doting care only made him more
vigorous as he planned his future. Fanny's cooking was healthful,
the orphan's laughter a diversion. His daughters and son were a
blessing, but he knew the love and devotion from Jane had been

the thread.

Speaking at the breakfast table, Grayton smiled up at his family. "Well, I am vigorous and fit once more, thanks to all of you it is time I return home to Rosewood Park."

Margaret nodded. "Indeed, sir."

"I think it a good plan for you to remain here, Margaret – that is, if you wish it," he said. "Miss Stewart, I take it you will look in on me every day?"

Jane blushed, "Oh, indeed my lord."

"Papa," said Mary, "must we return to London?"

Lizzy and Victoria stopped eating and stared at their father.

"Only if you wish it, daughters, but I've grown so accustomed to your lively banter I hardly think I can continue to grow healthier without you."

"Well, for my part, Papa, I wish to remain with you," said Lizzy.

"I shall miss Aunt Catherine," said Mary. "She has written that she misses us all very much." She glanced at Victoria. "Living in the country suits me, but perhaps London society is of your choosing, Vic. What have you to say?"

"Oh, most definitely, I choose to stay with you, Papa. Moreover, Miss Stewart has promised to show me her most excellent embroidery patterns – I so loved the peacock on black."

"Very well, then, it is settled. I am to be surrounded by the most beautiful women in the world."

"Sir," said Henry finishing the last of his coffee, "I am most anxious to be about helping William finish the new road. Highways have always fascinated my imagination, sir. I know plenty about them already. What is more, I have a plan that will near double our tenant farmer's deliveries if we but put another road into London from the north ..."

Grayton looked at his son in astonishment. "Why, indeed," he stood. "When once we are returned home, you must show me your plans."

* * *

The short journey from the Orphanage to Rosewood Park was pleasant enough. However, the carriage was a tight one with Lizzy, Mary and Victoria squeezed in on one side chattering and giggling at this and that and Henry and Lord Grayton with their backs to the horses. Henry, now excited beyond his happiest dreams, fidgeted in his seat anxious to pull out his many plans and drawings for the new north road out of Alton and proudly show them to his father.

* * *

As Lord Grayton's carriage pulled into the Rosewood Park's portico, every servant was standing in line to welcome the family home, at long last. There were smiles and gleeful chatter from everyone as his lordship climbed from the carriage.

"Oh, indeed, it is good to be home ..." said Grayton with a smile.

But even before he could utter another word, Lizzy, Mary and Victoria bounded past him and Henry as they rushed into the house jabbering and giggling tossing their wraps and hats to the waiting servants. "Oh, it is good to be home!" shouted Lizzy. As fast as a whirlwind the sisters were up the stairs to their rooms leaving Lord Grayton and Henry standing by the carriage.

"Well, sir," said Hall his butler, "I will speak for everyone here. We are most pleased and blest that you and Master Henry are home safe and sound."

All the servants cheered with their own well wishes.

Henry smiled. "Oh, thank you so much, thank you. Yes, he looked around with a grand smile. "It is good to be home."

"Indeed it is," said Lord Grayton as he eyed the grounds of his beloved Park. "There are no words ..."

Henry took his father's arm. "Come along, Father."

* * *

The very next morning as Lord Grayton sat in his study, he took a moment to savour the extraordinary view from his window. "Ah, yes, it is a very beautiful day, indeed." A certain quiet serenity seemed to flow through his veins, a new calm reigned over Rosewood Park—his children were no longer bickering with one another, Margaret was at peace with her medicine, Henry had become all that he had hoped for.

"Father," said Henry coming into the room, "am I interrupting your repose, sir?"

Grayton swivelled in his chair. "Of course not my boy, do join me."

"Thank you."

"So, Henry, I am anxious to see your work on this new road in Alton."

Henry puffed up. "Well, I am anxious for you to see the plans."

"Bring them," said Grayton as he stood, "let us go to the window for a good look."

Henry had his satchel in one hand and drawings tucked under his arm. "Oh, very good, sir."

Standing at the sideboard, Henry spread his drawings out and eagerly began engaging his father. "And sir, when I presented the plan to William he was amazed at the possibilities." Henry grinned. "He was astounded that the thought had never occurred to him earlier. Oh, it will take a bridge, but that should not be a problem. I love the idea of building one, sir."

Looking down at the pencil sketches, Grayton nodded in almost disbelief. "Well done, Henry, well done. I will have our London accountant come up with some figures."

Puffing up, Henry nodded. "Indeed, Father. I think they will favour my recommendations."

Grayton walked to the window and glanced out. "So, you have loved building roads, you never shared that with me before."

"Father, I've been away at Eton, and you've been distant."

"Indeed," he turned from the window, "but I am here now."

Henry glanced up at the chandelier, "Indeed you are, sir." He stood. "Father, I need your advice ... the most important decisions thus far in my life."

Grayton remained standing, thinking, listening ...

"Sir, I wish to marry Sarah."

His lordship's face grew sombre. "I thought as much." Turning from the window, he sighed heavily. "Henry, you know the morals and manners of the wealthy, our attitudes, our social standing, our rank in society. You know very well The King and Queen are very much the standard bearers of such etiquette, and breaches thereof. To take a wife, you must first secure their Majesties' blessings. I am on your side, Henry, but you know the King can be extremely difficult at times. The Queen is far more lenient on affairs of the heart."

"Indeed, sir, when Her Majesty came to see you just a few weeks past, it was she who offered us faith. 'Never give up hope,' she said."

"Indeed, she would have said such a thing," he sighed. "Well, tomorrow I am to leave for London, Henry. I have been summoned by the King. I am assuming he wishes to see for himself my restored good health, as I do theirs."

"Will you speak to them for me, Father?"

"I will."

Chapter 27 – The Earl Delights the King and Queen

The following day Lord Grayton climbed into his waiting carriage and tipped his hat to his son.

Henry knew just how important his father's visit to the King and Queen was. Indeed, his very future depended on the King's mood. "God's speed, Father."

It was just before twilight when Grayton's carriage ambled into London, and he made straightaway to the Palace. He was escorted into the private chamber of His Majesty's. The elegant room was aglow with candelabras, and the exquisite cut-crystal chandeliers' prisms shed light and shadows about the quiet space. He stood near the hearth warming his hands.

It was little time when both the King and Queen entered.

Bowing deeply, Grayton felt honoured at being allowed a private meeting with them.

The Queen hurried to his side. "Oh, my dear Grayton, how good it is to see you looking in health. And to think the last time I saw you I thought it to be my last."

"Indeed," said the King, "my wife stood at your deathbed but a fortnight ago. I cannot tell you how shocked and saddened I was by the news."

"Indeed, sir, it has been a shocking misfortune. One I wish never to endure again."

"Shock and pain to us as well."

"Yes, sir, and I heard you suffered with the influenza and for that I am sorry."

Her Majesty nodded. "Oh, yes, Grayton, he did suffer but was healed by your daughter, Lady Margaret. We will forever remember her devotedness."

Lord Grayton held a grim smile. "My daughter, Lady Margaret, wants to become a physician it seems. A rather crude endeavour, however …

Her Majesty's chin lifted. "Well, Grayton, she is very well

suited to such a position. She healed my husband and Lady Catherine. I must say not so crude in saving lives."

Grayton nodded, hiding a smile. "Indeed, madam, I shall tell her of your most excellent opinion."

"And I must say her companion, Miss Stewart, did a rather wonderful thing healing Lady Catherine as well. We shall not forget her either. The two make a splendid duo."

"Splendid duo?" said the King. "Well, call them what you may, but they must return to me when I am not feeling well. I demand it." He turned to Grayton. "Take a seat, you look all in."

His lordship nodded. "Indeed, sir. It was a long ride."

"I thought so." His Majesty joined him on the sofa nearest the hearth. "So, tell me, Grayton what else brings you?"

The Earl looked straight into His Majesty's eyes. "You know me too well, sir. Yes, there is another reason I am here; a reason far more important than anything else thus far in my life." Straightening his shoulders, he took a deep breath. "I am seeking your approval on my intended nuptials to Miss Jane Stewart."

The Queen shifted in her seat. "But of course, Miss Jane Stewart. The young lady who nursed His Majesty back to health." She glanced at the King. "You thought highly of her, sir."

"Indeed," he said rubbing his chin. "Ah, yes, henceforth we shall call her Sophie ... the one with yellow hair."

Grayton looked perplexed. "Sir, I do not know her as Sophie. I only know her as Miss Jane Stewart."

"Yes, well she has a twin, Juliet, who has yet to make herself known to me. I have waited a very long time to see them together again."

Grayton glanced at the floor. *The King is going into one of his strange moods again ... talking nonsense.* "Ah, sir, Miss Jane Stewart is my intended bride, if you so deem it. She is from a family with no money, no connections, and with no one to recommend her to a higher class."

"Is that so?" said the King.

"Miss Stewart's sister, Anne Whitmore and her husband, William were the ones I chose to school my son, Henry. Both Miss Stewart and her sister were abandoned at the Holybourne Orphanage ... at their birth, sir."

The Queen smiled. "Oh, yes, we know. We know a great deal more than you do."

Not exactly sure what she meant, Grayton nodded. "Indeed, Your Majesty."

"Is that all you have to present to us, Grayton?" said the

King.

With a deep sigh, he nodded. "Allow me to speak for my beloved son Henry on his behalf. He wishes to marry Miss Jane Stewart's niece, Miss Sarah Whitmore."

"Sarah? The young lady who saved you both as you lay dying along the London Road in Holybourne?" said the King looking smug.

The Queen glanced at her husband with a smile. "Why, George, I am stunned to hear you are aware of *her* story."

The King, rubbing his backside, chided his wife. "Oh, madam, you are not the only clever one in the room. Oh, yes, some may doubt my reasoning, but I have a fine memory and a very inquisitive nature." He motioned for Grayton to come front and centre. "And I remember very well the night you came to me saying there were two shooting stars crossing paths when Henry was born. And I told you to go find your son's mate – Oh, I remember the twin-birth omen very well, my friend.

"Grayton, I will be celebrating my fiftieth birthday next month. You shall come to the celebration with your family and Miss Stewart. Henry may bring this Miss Sarah and her mother and father. I shall have my answer for you then, at the celebration—in the grand ballroom." He glanced at his wife with a smirk.

The Queen gave no hint of approval or disapproval to the matrimonial match between the couples. She was the formidable one of the two, however, and without her approval, Grayton was doomed, and he knew it.

Grayton bowed. "Your Majesty's, thank you." Removing from the room, he held a brave face, but in his heart of hearts, he knew he had overstepped his boundaries—asking a personal favour on too grand a scale, perhaps.

The King's reputation was already in question, he and the Queen knew that well. And now to announce the proposal and acceptance of an Earl *and* his son's marriage to commoners far beneath the strict social ladder—well, it was extreme.

But the royal couple had a plan.

On his return to the orphanage, Grayton sat in his barouche as it moved through the south gate of London. The air was thick with the possibility of rain. Heavy dark clouds swirled just above the Tower of London, brackish choppy waves slapped about the shores of the Thames. His heart was sad, for he was most certain that the King's response would be one of denial. *O God, what have I done to my family, my dearest Jane, and the Whitmores? But then again, why would His Majesty pick such a happy occa-*

sion to not give his blessing?

When his carriage pulled up to the orphanage gate, there stood Jane on the porch, surrounded by her orphans. And there next to her, happily situated, stood Henry and Sarah, smiling. A warm happiness filled his troubled heart. *Indeed like sunshine sundering a rain cloud.*

"Hello, hello," Jane's beautiful white teeth gleamed as she hurried to greet him.

Stepping from the carriage, he took her hand. "Come let us gather before the hearth. I have many plans to share."

Though still walking a bit slow and leaning heavily on his walking stick, Grayton entered the study to find his daughters, Mary and Victoria working with a little child stitching embroidery. Lizzy huddled in the corner petting the big grey cat. Margaret was tending the bruised knee of one little boy.

"I have good news to share, tomorrow morn we shall be off to Poplar Grove for holiday. There is room enough for all, the children, Fanny, yes, everyone is welcome."

Lizzy lit up with a great smile holding up the cat. "Can we bring this old fellow, Papa?"

"He shall ride on top." He turned and faced everyone in the room. "I have another matter I wish to share with you, now that we are all gathered together. We have all been invited to celebrate with His Majesty on his 50th birthday, the fourth day of June."

Chapter 28 – A Royal Invitation

Lord Grayton was alone in his study when a courier rang. His butler, Hall, entered.

"Sir, a Royal letter."

The Rt Honourable The Earl of Grayton.
Dear Lord Grayton,
Their Royal Majesties, King George III and Queen Charlotte, invite you to a ball to celebrate His Majesty's fiftieth birthday. At Norfolk-House, St. James Square, London, 4 June
HRH, King George III.

There was a scribble at the bottom, in Her Majesty's own hand:

Grayton, the King and I do not soon forget Miss Stewart's devotion to my husband during his illness and the kindness shown by the Whitmores. Regarding your nuptials ... well, I am never certain anymore of His Majesty's thoughts ...
HRH Charlotte

Grayton gazed out his window, rain pattered lightly against the thick, bubbled-glassed pane. From its grey light, he read the Royal invitation again. *How very prophetic that the two sisters should be together on such an occasion.* The inevitable reality of the situation he created had to be dealt with, and soon.

What if the King denied my request to marry? This would undoubtedly be too painful an exposure, too injurious to two such beautiful, sweet-natured women, Jane and Sarah. And what would they think of me allowing such discord? He was caught between loyalty and love.

"Sir," said Hall, "Miss Stewart has arrived."

"Bring her, please."

Within a short time, Jane entered.

"How was the ride from Holybourne, Jane?"

"Oh, the ride went very well, sir." She removed her wrap. "I received word that you needed me immediately, sir." She smiled, her cheeks rosy, her eyes moist and attentive. Her hair slicked back into a neat bun, and about her shoulders a pink scarf.

He poked the smouldering logs and blew at a few red embers. The flames quickly licked up, and again the fire caught hold, snapping and crackling. He stood in front of it, contemplatively watching the flames, fanning them. He handed her the Royal invitation.

"Why, the ball sounds wonderful, my lord." She read on, "I see Her Majesty has written an additional note ..."

"Indeed."

She read it, a puzzled look spread across her face.

"You shall accompany me, Jane. Sarah will accompany Henry, along with William and Anne. I must tell you that while in London speaking with their Majesty's I, I requested their approval to marry you."

She dropped her hands. "Their approval?" Stepping back, she held a sternest look. "This is your proposal of marriage, to me, sir? And you asked them first?" She looked in him in the eye. "After all these years, my devotion to you ..." she took a seat, burying her head in her hands. "It would have been exceedingly polite had you only spoke with me first, in the proper fashion regarding marriage, sir."

Grayton puffed up. "And why is that, Jane? You know I have always loved you above all others. Why, I did not see the need." He moved to the window and glanced out. "Do you have any idea the precarious position I am placing my family and myself by marrying you, and by allowing Henry to marry your niece—particularly one with a deformity?"

Jane stood, her cheeks now colourless. There was a chill in her voice. "Indeed, such a deformity. As for my niece, sir, she may marry whom she chooses. At the moment, my lord, I have no plans on marrying anyone. My first love is to my abandoned children. They hold me in the highest regard. They are truly the ones in a precarious position, and I shall not leave them. Goodday to you, sir." She stopped. "One more word, my lordship, why did you leave Henry with Whitmores' to be raised with morals and manners? It quite escapes me?" She grabbed her shawl and hurried out the door.

"Jane, Jane, wait." He caught the tip of her cape, snatching it from her shoulders.

"You may keep it, sir." She fumed.

"Jane, you don't understand the complexities ..."

"No, sir, I do not, nor do I wish to understand such a cold, calculating affair." Now standing next to the carriage, she opened the door herself and climbed in. "And you expect me to attend a grand ball in honour of His Majesty and hang on his every word until he so chooses to anoint me with his blessings to allow common blood to pollute your royal circle?"

His face drained. "Jane, you quite mistake the situation ..."

"And, sir, if he so chooses to deny the nuptials? What am I to do, bow politely and smile?"

She tapped the ceiling with her hand. "Move on."

The Earl stared after her carriage as it moved down the road. "Well, well, now."

* * *

Grayton found his son, Henry, in a quiet part of the library, tracing. He was detailing a bridge span for the new road when he entered.

Standing, he nodded. "Good afternoon, Father."

Grayton glanced down at his son's work. "Most excellent pen-and-ink sketches, you draw marvellously well, Henry."

"Thank you, sir." He remained standing. "Sir?"

"Do sit down, Henry. I have news from Their Majesty's."

"Regarding Sarah and me, sir?"

"Yes," he glanced around, "is she still here?"

"She left just this morning for Alton, sir."

"Well, then, we shall just have to go there." He pulled out his timepiece. "Tomorrow, we have not the time today."

"Indeed, Father, dare I ask their Majesty's decision?"

He handed him the Royal invitation.

Reading it, Henry looked puzzled. "What does this mean,

Father?"

"It means that His Majesty will inform us of his decision to grant his approval for you to marry Sarah at the ball. And now we must speak with Sarah and her family."

Henry frowned. "So, we are not *assured* of his approval then?"

"I am sorry to say, son, no."

"Hmm." Henry sunk down into his chair. "Well, Father, I should not be shocked, but we must prepare Sarah and her family. Our King can be odd betimes."

"Indeed," said Grayton dropping his head.

"Miss Stewart, Father. Have you spoken to her as well?"

He nodded. "I certainly did, Henry."

"And ...?"

"Oh, she had a good bit to say."

* * *

Grayton and Henry left Rosewood Park for Alton the following afternoon. Muddy pools of rain etched the road ahead, a slight trace of fresh cool air found its way into their carriage.

Henry watched his father who sat huddled in the corner, his eyes closed, his gloved hands resting on his lap. An occasional deep sigh escaping now and again. "Is there something amiss, Father? You are in deep thought, it seems."

"Nothing more than a miscalculation, Henry," he sat up. "Miss Stewart read the invitation as well."

"This miscalculation, Father, it is of your making?"

"Henry, it is possible that His Majesty could very easily refuse my request to marry, refuse you as well. We must be prepared for such an eventuality."

* * *

As the Grayton carriage approached the Whitmores', everyone hurried out into the courtyard to greet them, except Anne.

Patting Henry on the back, William looked delighted. "Well, we are pleased at the unexpected visit. Do come in."

Sarah took Henry's hand. "I have been home only a day," she whispered, "have you missed me so much that you come again?" she giggled, her cheeks pink.

"My lord," said William, "tell us, what brings you?"

"Some worthy news, William."

Anne entered, her smile stiff; her manner cool.

William gestured toward the parlour. "Please come in by the fire."

Grayton nodded and followed everyone into the room. "Thank you, William. I have come to share with you an invitation to the King's birthday ball. Queen Charlotte personally invited you, Anne and Sarah." He handed the invitation to Anne.

She briefly glanced at it. "My lord, I am very much aware of the invitation." Handing it back, she did not look at him. Disappointment was not well hidden on her face.

Grayton glanced at Anne. "I take it Jane has spoken to you then?"

"She has."

William looked confused. "Is something amiss, Anne?"

Grayton shook his head. "I most recently spoke with their Majesties." He glanced at Henry and Sarah. "I asked for their blessings on taking Jane as my wife and for Henry to wed Sarah. To be blunt, the King must sanction both our marriages." He stiffened. "He will announce his decision at the ball."

Henry squeezed Sarah's hand. "The King can be quite difficult, Sarah. He may not shed his blessings on ..."

"Your choice of a wife, Henry," said Anne warmly. "Let me assure you, my lords, our daughter and my sister are not to be trifled with. I have not spoken to William regarding your intentions, both your intentions." She looked at Grayton. "I have just learned of Jane's refusal to you, my lord."

Sarah gaped. "Of what are you speaking, Mother? You have me confused."

Henry took Sarah's hand. "Sarah, I have loved you, it seems, forever, please understand."

"But if the King forbids such an affiliation then what?" said Anne. "I will spare my daughter what my sister has so wisely decided to do."

Sarah gaped. "Mother, tell me, what has Aunt Jane decided to do?"

Grayton's head hung low.

Henry spoke up, "Your Aunt Jane understands the societal consequences of Father and me, if we choose to marry beneath our rank without His Majesty's approval. The snubs, the deliberate exclusions; the King can make life very difficult, Sarah. But, these are not heavy concerns that would deter you, I should think. I pray they would not, for I intend on marrying you despite the King's objections ... if you wish it."

He handed her the invitation. "You and your family are invited to His Majesty's birthday ball ... and that is where he will give his decision."

"Well, then, it seems there is a chance he will deny us, Henry," said Sarah looking hurt.

Anne put her arm around her daughter. "Dearest, I only want to spare you the pain and humiliation that may come of all this. You have been innocently put in the pathway of a most scandalous affair. I am now most grieved over it." She glared at Grayton.

Henry took her hand. "But, Anne, is it not such a coincidence that Sarah and I were born on the same day as the King? Were there not two stars in the heavens crossing paths at our birth? Surely you cannot so easily dismiss such omens, good omens. You do believe it is our destiny?"

"Henry," said his lordship, "we must leave these good people to decide their own destinies."

Henry pulled Sarah to his side. "I am not shaken in my desires for taking you as my wife, Sarah."

Anne pulled her from his side. "Your father is correct, Henry. Please leave us – us *commoners*."

Chapter 29 – The King's Birthday – London, 4 June 1788

Rains came early that morning, but by noon the sun had broken through, and from the warm cobblestone streets a vapour was misting away, in wile fashion, exsiccating fast into the breezes that drove the dark, thunderous storm clouds swiftly from the city, along with it, the nasty odours.

His Majesty stood from his bath, full naked, front-wise to the window while the warm summer zephyrs blew lightly through the Royal bath chamber tickling his rotund buckskin belly-wrap. And as he tossed his Royal locks about his shoulders, the King, being very contented, happily cried out, "Ah wife, this could not be a better day to be born!"

He loved to bathe in the warmth of summer, and took great delight in splashing his wife many times over as she tried reading to him Shakespeare's *Romeo and Juliet*. She enjoyed the banter, but all the while, happy that he was acting civilly rather than being in an outrage; or worse yet, running naked through the thorny rose gardens.

Now finally dried, the King paused at his wife's reading. "Is there not a Sophie that helps Juliet in that story, wife?"

"No, dear," she mused, "I have not found a Sophie that matches with Juliet in any of his stories. Perhaps you are thinking of our newly anointed, long-forgotten cousins, Sophie and Juliet? Born on your birthday, some thirty plus years ago, perhaps they shall be here tonight for your celebration?"

"Ah, yes, little golden-haired Sophie and dearest Juliet with glossy bright red hair," said the King with a smile. "I could never forget them."

"And to think, my selection of Romeo and Juliet should evoke such memories, dear." She pressed the book to her bosom.

"I remember." Moving his head this way and that, he adjusted his undergarments. Tugging his loincloth, fussing, "Oh, they always pinch ill to my buttocks." He glanced into the long mirror and frowned. "Well, come along, wife, I have something I must show you."

He was as happy as his step was light. Servants scurried by his side, grabbing towels hoping His Majesty's underwear covered all things concerned. Courtiers, who happened to be in the hallway, cleared a path wondering if the King was on one of his wayward *walkabouts* again. They watched the half-dressed monarch's entourage hustle by, followed by their many hounds scrambling down the hallway in utter delight at their good fortune for they had escaped the water dunks the King so enjoyed.

"Come along, Charlotte," he said as he hurried down the hallway rattling the crystal chandeliers as he walked. Coming to a stop just outside the private residence, he gestured toward the portrait of Manfred. "There you have it, Charlotte," said the King, looking quite pleased. "Look here."

Trying to catch her breath, the Queen stood looking up at the oil of Manfred when along came the efficacious Mr Pepper, Recorder of Antiquities.

"Antiquities fellow, come this way and tell Her Majesty who this is."

"Dear," said Charlotte incredulously, "I know who it is. It is Viscount Southsussex, your cousin, for it was I who pointed it out to *you*, evening last."

Peter Pepper looked at the King, seemingly too petrified to speak.

Standing in his underwear, the King repeated, "Fellow, I say, take out your little Book of Antiquities there and read aloud what is written about him. I want to hear again … what you told me earlier."

"Your Majesty," Mr Pepper bowed stiffly, took the book from under his arm and opened it to the very page. Clearing his parched throat, he began: "Sir Manfred Curl." His words, coming out dry and unintelligible he repeated, "Southsussex, born 1740, died 1766, married Lady Agnes (nee) Moore, bore twin daughters, June 4, infants Lady Sophie and Lady Juliet, born into intrigue, disappeared at birth. Lady Agnes died in labour." He then closed the book and stared directly at the wall before him witnessing the half-naked king rub his belly. *Dear me.*

The Queen smiled. "Hmm, the twins disappeared, did they?"

"Hold your tongue, Charlotte. Do not utter another word upon the matter for I have solved the puzzle myself." He nudged her. "Cannot you imagine to what puzzle I am alluding?"

She giggled. "Indeed I do," she tweaked his chin, "my clever husband."

"I say, Pepper, henceforth you shall be Royal Recorder of all Palaces in the realm."

Pepper staggered back, stumbled and mumbled aloud at his good fortune. "Thank you, Your Majesty, thank you, thank you, thank you." Bowing his departure, his butt hit the wall.

Queen Charlotte and the King broke out in hysterical fits of laughter.

Lady Catherine came from around the corner, startled to find His Majesty with little clothing. Curtsying, she covered her blushing face with her fan. "Excuse me, Your Majesty."

"Lady Catherine, who is this man?" The King pointed to Manfred, ignoring her stares at his buckskin belly. "Well then, come now, who is it?"

"Why, Your Majesty, that is Manfred Curl, Southsussex, your cousin."

"Precisely," he said as he took his wife's arm and began the long jog back down the Great Hall to the bath chamber, his butt-cheeks wiggling wildly at the royal romp.

"I must be absolutely sure to your meaning, dear," said the Queen.

"Very well," he whispered at length into her ear. "Just wait, wife, until this evening during my birthday ball, for you shall be a long time coming to match this surprise."

Smiling the Queen glanced out the window. *I wager Grayton to be the one surprised.*

Chapter 30 – 4 June – At the King's Ball

Oliver, the footman at Rosewood Park, stepped forward, opened the carriage door, and bowed to Grayton. "My lord," he said politely.

His lordship exchanged pleasantries and boarded the carriage. "Well, I suppose I must attend the ball, Oliver." He sighed deeply. "But I suppose this evening shall pass as all others have."

"Indeed, sir." Oliver closed the door.

Grayton reached into his vest pocket and brought out the pin-portrait of King George that the Queen pinned on him when he was near death. Within hours his carriage passed through the gates of London and over the Thames. The clip-clop of his horses' hooves echoed sharply on the bridge stones. It was early evening yet, and the bright yellow sun was just setting behind a mix of blue swirling pinkish sort of clouds.

He glanced out at the sky, "Blue as Jane's eyes. How remarkable, the warm silver of the clouds matches her hair precisely."

Arriving at St James Square, he stiffened. There were many, many coaches, horses, and people of all sorts mingling about the walk. Commoners, without a personal invitation, could come and see His Majesty, if they too were born on this day, the King's birthday. They could take a bit of food and drink, and wander about at will. However, when the music began, they were warned, they would be allowed only to watch the privileged Royal society disembark from their carriages.

Grayton stepped down from the carriage where the admiring masses were assembled. The people eyed everything from his hat to his boots. Envy and wishful glances were written on each face, clean and dirty alike. He looked directly into the eyes of these wishful thinkers, men with crooked, rotted teeth, emaciated women bald from worry, and the many other, healthy happy ones—all those who were lucky enough to have been born this day. The upper classes had their share of cripples, loveless souls, bitter and embattled soldiers of fortune, and some called them spent idlers.

Before Grayton entered the *privileged section*, he glanced back and found dancers winding their way through the people, from under the many tables, through small open spaces, from among the many ornate designed columns in the Great Ballroom. There were gold ribbons and fine silk cloths streaming everywhere, Royal banners, and on the floor were exquisite Oriental rugs, matted wool, and matted cane rugs—all in bright blazing colours.

Over against the far wall, stood long, ornately carved serving tables, and upon each sat huge casks of wine with candied fruit, apricots, nuts, and sugared dates surrounding each. On one large black round table in the Great Ballroom's very centre, sat a huge roasted hog's head decorated with a fine cloth mask in Royal blue.

The sights, sounds, and smells quite held him spellbound from such a display of food and associations. He nodded to a few of his acquaintances from the old London society.

The horns blew suddenly. The King's birthday celebration would soon begin. The Great Ballroom doors would close. The onlookers were no longer afforded the luxury of *peeping* into the Great Hall, they would be left only to hear the music echoing out into the streets.

"Papa," cried Lizzy as she ran to greet him, "at last I have found you. Mary, Victoria, and I have been sitting with the Queen's Maids-of-Honour," she pointed, "just there."

He smiled at her. "Ah, my little star, so you have." Glancing around, he frowned. "But, where is your Aunt Catherine?"

She shrugged. "I have no idea, Papa."

"Well, you were to be under her protection while in London."

"Sir, we have not seen Aunt Catherine for a good many days. We have been chaperoned by Lady Marlsborough ... the Queen insisted."

"Insisted?"

"Indeed, Papa. Lady Marlsborough sent her carriage. I must admit we have been delightfully entertained the entire evening."

Grayton nodded. "Well, you will be returning with me after the ball."

Shrugging, Lizzy giggled, "We are having a marvellous time of it, Papa." Her eyes glistened. "The ball will be magnificent, Papa."

"Oh, yes, I am quite sure of it."

Lizzy took his hand. "Come then, Papa, Victoria and Mary

are just there."

"I will join you shortly, Elizabeth."

* * *

The King and Queen were introduced with much trumpeting of horns. King George loved the attention from his well-wishers. The people clearly adored him. The Queen was overjoyed at her husband's good humour. All her fifteen children moved along in the procession, most were happy of the scene, save the eldest son, Prince George. He promised one sibling never to repeat attending such a silly ball. "Mother and Father are making such a stupid spectacle of themselves. Who cares when Father was born."

Hundreds of gold sheers billowed, banners and ribbons fluttered. Their Majesties' crowns glistened and sparkled with diamonds, rubies, and pearls.

The sight quite took Grayton's breath. "Such pomp and pageantry, a fairy tale, indeed," he glanced around the room searching for his daughters. Their Majesty's positioned themselves at their respective thrones. The King was first to sit, then the Queen. The music began at the King's nod and within a moment's notice there came entertainers deftly swinging swords, jugglers tossing hand-painted balls high in the air, flimsy dressed maidens danced, and magic tricks abounded everywhere.

The air was filled with hundreds of scented candles, all set in clever places to illuminate and lending the room romantic. Night was full upon the Great Hall. The fine ladies and gentlemen moved slowly around the room, nodding, splashing a bit of wine, laughing in fake spurts.

Being unusually warm, Grayton strolled out onto the balcony. Glancing up into the beautiful evening air, he spotted a shooting star as it glowed in the royal blue heavens. "I suppose shooting stars are for wishing upon." He bowed his head in respectful obedience and thought of Jane. He felt the coolness of London's night air swirl lightly about as he made his wish. He listened to the sounds of a city slowly unwinding. Below he heard the noise of a gatekeeper's key and chain, the slackened pace of an evening horse at his cart, a lonely dog's bark. The music stopped, Grayton heard the King's voice and returned to the Great Ballroom. He thought of his daughters. "Ah, I shall find my little lambs shortly."

Taking the Queen's arm, the King stood. The music faded,

the dancers wound to a stop, the clinking of glasses ceased.

"Father, there you are, sir," whispered Henry dabbing his forehead with his handkerchief. "I have been searching for you."

"Indeed, Henry, I have been here. Have you seen your sisters?"

"Sir," he took his arm, "that is why I have come. Follow me, I have something to share."

"It must wait, the King is about to speak."

"No, Father, you must come at once."

The two walked out onto the balcony. "This way, sir," said Henry as he hurriedly led his father down the long concourse and into an open courtyard below.

"Henry, you must explain what you are about?"

"Sir, I saw Lizzy, Victoria and Mary being hustled, if you will, by the King's guards. Lizzy was crying, sir."

"What? Why, I just spoke to her moments ago ..." Glancing around he took Henry's arm. "Take me to where you last saw them."

As they tried to make way through the surging crowd, it grew impossible for them to go any farther. "Henry, we must wait until His Majesty speaks and then we will find them."

* * *

The King took a few steps, took a sip from his silver chalice and turned to those assembled. "I have some rather startling news to share with you." He gulped the remainder of his wine. "While perusing the Hallway of Antiquities most recently, I caught a glimpse of my distant cousin, Manfred Curl. His portrait was hung in an obscure place—at the end of an old hall, if you can believe such a thing." He glanced at his wife and smiled. "To think, at one time he was called ill-fit. A man ill-fit to serve his people, but it was all a ploy to fool the French in the war. He was a spy, after all, a hero long forgotten, perhaps by most, never known.

"Her Majesty had it dusted and hung in its rightful place ... at my door." He scanned the yawning audience. "But you think all this means nothing to you?" He smiled. "But, I now have discovered his twin daughters. A difficult birth, as their mother, Agnes, died labouring them. They were born in a small hamlet and left in an orphanage far south of here, Holybourne—how fitting a name. His daughters, my dearest cousins, Lady Sophie and Lady

Juliet, were near identical, except one had sun-gold hair and the other fire red hair.

"My cousin Manfred, Southsussex, and his wife were involved in intrigue for the glorification of England, but alas, the campaign failed, and he returned to the palace with the children, paying a secret visit here. He was to visit me the very next day and leave his daughters here for safe keeping. But, he could not bear to be apart from his family and left with them, bringing along their governess, all under disguise, of course.

"Later I was informed that my heroic Cousin Curl, died in battle. His daughters were given to a French General's wife, who soon tired of them. Their governess, realising the jeopardy of the infants, stole away in the night bringing them to English soil. For safety, she hid them away in an obscure orphanage, where they were raised. The governess, still frightened that the General's wife would find them, remained hidden for a good many years.

"Most recently the governess felt it safe to bring this news to me. And with help from Lady Catherine Bute, I soon learned of my missing family."

Nodding with a smile, Catherine fanned her warm face, trying not so very hard at masking her important deed. "It is a pleasure, Your Majesty, to be in your service."

"Indeed the twins have been brought to the Palace to be reunited with the Queen and me. Soon they shall be presented at Court ... their false identity? Well, all along it has been Miss Jane Stewart and her sister, Mrs Anne Whitmore."

The audience clapped in wonder, glancing back and forth with smiles and nods—not the least bit interested at such a find, for they were more interested in the feast and fine wine that awaited them.

"Find Grayton," said the King whispering to his wife. "Indeed, Lady Sophie and Lady Juliet have been sequestered here in secret so as to make them presentable to their lessers. They will make their grand entrance this very evening in the splendour they so deserve."

"Where is Grayton?" he whispered, becoming impatient.

"Oh, he will soon be at your side, my dear." She sighed with a contented smile. "Indeed, sir. What a pleasure it will be to witness his happiness. Now all his cares are for nought. John and Henry can marry as they choose."

"Indeed, I have finally found the best sort of way in returning such favours to my closest friend, confidant, and advisor." Glancing over the weary-eyed assemblage, he noted his children had left the room. "Oh, how predictable they are, Charlotte."

"Indeed. I think we should have lopped off their insolent little heads years ago, my dear."

The music suddenly began again, and the murmurs abounded in the crowd, had the King succumbed to another *episode*?

"Charlotte, where on earth is Grayton?"

Lady Catherine approached. "Your Majesty, may I have a word?"

He nodded. "You may."

"Well, it appears the French have succeeded once again."

Cocking his head, he glared at her. "What is the meaning of your words, Lady Catherine?"

"A trap, apparently. I would wager both Lady Juliet and Lady Sophie have been absconded by ill means—you know the French." She glanced around at the faces assembled about the room. "Someone in your court has passed on the identity of Sophie and Juliet."

The Queen stood. "That's impossible. From the very beginning, it was just the King and I who knew."

"Yes, that's right," he said.

Glancing around, Lady Catherine demurely fanned her face. "Privacy is in order, Your Majesties. I have some very important news to share."

Realizing the crowd had become impatient, the Queen instructed her ladies-in-waiting, "Feed them, wine them, pluck the strings for them."

The King gestured toward the side door. "Into my private room, then, Lady Catherine."

Now secured in His Majesty's private chamber, Lady Catherine took in a great breath. "Oh, Your Majesty, it is all true. General Lafayette reclaims the twins as his rightful daughters."

The King scratched his head. "Lafayette? Stop this at once, you are speaking in riddles. The only General Lafayette I know is old, defeated, and up to his ruffled collar in debt."

"Oh, indeed, Your Majesty, the very one, and no doubt the very reason, money. My informants say Mademoiselle Lafayette claims Lady Sophie and Lady Juliet as her own. During the war, Manfred, in order to spare his life, gave away his twins to her."

"Preposterous," Looking over at his wife, the King sank down into his chair with a grunt, "They are grown women. What would she want with them now?"

"Lady Catherine, explain your meaning," said the Queen.

"Well, I was told the twins were newborns when their English governess stole them away one night in Paris and smuggled them back to England. Word has it, Mademoiselle Lafayette has been searching for them ever since."

"Who told you all that nonsense?" demand the Queen. "I must know at once."

"Lady Catherine continued to fan her warm face." I, I am not a liberty to disclose his identity ..."

"*His* identity?"

"Will someone explain to me what is going on?" said the King.

Queen Charlotte glared at Lady Catherine. "What part do you play in this, Lady Catherine?"

"Oh, Your Majesty, I've played no part in their disappearance. No part, whatsoever. I assure you."

"Is that so?" said the Queen as she whispered into the King's ear.

An odd look spread across his face. "And I would suppose a King's ransom is now in order for their return?"

"Oh, Your Majesty, I would not know of such sordid details."

"Oh, indeed not," said the Queen. "Lady Catherine, you are not telling us all that you know. Why did you not come to us earlier with this news? Come now, you must confess your involvement in this scheme, and at once or ..."

"Heads will roll," said the King.

"Oh, ma'am, I do not know one thing regarding their disappearance." She paused, "However, there is one such person who could possibly shed some light on this dastardly unfortunate affair."

"And who might that be?" said the Queen.

"Why, ma'am, Lord Grayton, of course. He was the last person to have seen the twins, alive."

Staring at her in disbelief, the Queen looked directly into her eyes. "And how would you have known such a fact, madam?"

Her face lost its colour, unfamiliar with the tone of Her Majesty's voice, she took in a breath. "Well, I am not at liberty to explain *just* how I know."

"You are now, Lady Catherine. Explain yourself this very instant."

Lady Catherine fanned her face, her eyes darting from the floor to the ceiling.

Pursing her lips, the Queen clapped her hands. "Explain yourself."

"Very well, the governess told me."

"The governess?" said the King.

"It is all true. Allow me to bring her here, Your Majesty. I shall go at once." She turned to leave.

The King barred her exit. "Not without my guards."

Lady Margaret had entered in the middle of the fracas and stood listening in disbelief.

"How much do they want, Catherine?" said the Queen.

Just then Grayton and Henry were escorted in.

Margaret hurried to her father's side. "I take it you have heard the terrible news, sir?"

With ashen face, he nodded. "I have."

She wiped her eyes and took Henry's hand. "Impossible," she whispered, choking up.

"Do not cry so, sister," he patted her hand. "She will pay for her deeds."

"Where is Lady Sophie and Juliet, Catherine?" said the King.

"I, I have not taken them anywhere, I swear it." She looked at Margaret and Henry pleadingly. "I do not know of what he speaks ... you must believe me."

"Oh, after all we have heard, we are to now believe you?" scoffed the Queen.

Henry shook his head. "Aunt Catherine, how could you?"

She waved her little lace handkerchief and turned to the King. "I told you, but you would not listen. Lafayette has them, and he has demanded a great ransom for their return."

Grayton gasped. Margaret dropped her head into her hands. Henry put his arm around her shoulder.

"Very well, then." Tugging on the rope pull, he asked for his Captain of the Household Troops.

The Troops entered the room. Captain Smith saluted. "Your Majesty, at your service."

"Captain, you will take £10,000 and this woman," he took Lady Catherine's arm, "and deliver her by sea to General Lafayette."

The stiff-lipped Captain nodded. "Indeed, Your Majesty."

The Troops encircled her.

"Catherine, these men will escort you to the French port of Calais," instructed the King. "They will remain at sea, not stepping on French soil. They will put you, and the money, on a small boat. Lady Sophie and Lady Juliet had better be in the boat at its return ... without you."

"Very well, Your Majesty." She dabbed her upper lip with her gloved hand. "But I will need a little time to arrange things ..."

"Time?"

"Oh, yes, sir. Though I know nothing of this sordid affair, I will use all my valuable insights and connections, for there are many, sir, to find them. Depend upon it. I shall get to the bottom of all this debauchery." Sensing victory in her argument, she proudly lifted her chin. "But, I will need a few days to sort all of this out."

"One day Catherine and that's the end of it," said the King.

Bowing low, her face cold, she finished with royal protocol and stood erect. "You have judged me unfairly, sir, and I shall prove it."

"I cannot wait, Catherine."

She turned to leave, took a few steps and then stopped. "Oh, Your Majesty, before I go, I must ask, am I to be paid for my work? For I have little in my purse and do not know how I should go about my business in securing the whereabouts of your nieces without a few coins to rattle about."

The Queen's face turned a deep red.

Glancing up at the chandelier, the King shook his head. "Oh, how short-sighted I have become. Would a hundred pounds suit you?"

Smiling, she tugged at her gloves. "Well ... Your Majesty, perhaps two-hundred then?" Picking up her fan, she snapped it open. "It is a chilling business, this hostage fracas, to be sure."

"Chilling, indeed," said the Queen.

Fanning her face, Lady Catherine spun on her heels, and without a final curtsy, left the room.

"Your Majesty, what am I to think?" said Grayton.

"Happy birthday, indeed!" The King stormed out of the ballroom with the Queen at his side. He called over his shoulder, "Come along, Grayton."

Grayton, Margaret and Henry followed.

Stomping his way along the hall, the King bellowed, "I might have guessed Catherine to be a traitor, what with her forever requesting more and more to live her ever extravagant, wasteful ways. Well, there's the end of it, and her in the bargain."

The Queen touched her lips. "Oh, dear me, her life, sir?"

He nodded with a sullen lip.

Abruptly stopping, she sighed deeply. "Sir, I wonder if there really is a General Lafayette?"

"Who gives a fig," said the King.

* * *

After securing her two hundred pounds in gold, Lady Catherine tied her purse to her waist and turned to her footman. "Have my carriage readied, Rufus, I must be in Alton before first light." Just before leaving the Palace, she glanced at herself in the hall mirror. "You are looking at a soon-to-be very wealthy lady."

"Yes, ma'am," said Rufus.

Kicking up her parasol, she sniffed the air. "Indeed."

Looking down from the King's private chamber window, Grayton shook his head as she climbed into her carriage. "May the devil take you."

* * *

Lady Catherine's carriage made good time as it rolled into Alton. The church spire clock struck four chimes. Light was just beginning to break dawn; the horses were lathered and breathing hard. Rufus jumped from the carriage and opened the door. "Madam, we have arrived."

She stepped from the carriage steps being careful not to soil the hem of her exquisite silk frock and continued to hold it just above her boots as she walked toward the stone steps leading to the church. "I want to be done with this business and out of here before the half-past chimes strike, Rufus."

"Oh, indeed, ma'am." He glanced up at the clock. "They should be here very soon."

"Bring me my purse. They must be assured I have the money or the family will not be released into my custody."

Rufus nodded and hurried to the carriage. Hurrying back, he was all a breath, his eyes wide and weird. "I searched everywhere," he said with a dry throat, "but it was not there."

"What? It must be there, I left it on the seat right next to where I sat." She hurried off the steps and headed for the carriage. "It was too heavy ..."

Rufus hurried alongside. "There is no one about. Why, not even a cock crows."

Reaching the carriage, Lady Catherine cared less about mussing her frock as she climbed in and began frantically pulling at the seats, sweeping the floor with her white-gloved hands, clearing her eyes that she may see in the darkness. Now stepping out onto dew-wet grass, she spoke aloud, "When we stopped at the White Swan ... I did not go in. My purse was by my side the entire time." She walked around the carriage kicking the grass. "Perhaps it fell out when I stepped from the carriage."

"No, I have searched everywhere," said Rufus. "It is nowhere to be found."

"Good God, what am I to say to them?" She covered her mouth shaking her head in disbelief. "Without the money, they will be killed."

"You promised them men money, and we don't have it. We might be done away with as well."

She nodded. The clock struck half-past the hour.

"Hurry away then, you fool." Jumping into the carriage, she scolded Rufus for closing the door on her hem. "And take another road to the Palace. I must not be followed."

The carriage made way back down into the lowlands, though it would take two hours more to London, she was satisfied that no one was following.

"Well, I suppose every one of them will be done away with now." She snapped her fan open. "And to think all my plans are in a snit! And the lost money ... well, she shook her head, "Two hundred pounds is not such a great sum." She thought long and hard in the quietness of her carriage. The ride was bumpy and jolting as she braced herself with her foot on the opposite seat. "I am a clever woman, let me think what I must next do."

A great flash visited upon her brain as she sat forward. "But of course, that is precisely what I shall tell the King ... the cloth-headed silly old fool that he has become. Why, no one will be the wiser."

* * *

Two days had passed, and the very anxious King and Queen summoned the Graytons to their chamber. It was but little time when they were ushered in. The Queen stood at the hearth, her face pale.

Bowing, Grayton nodded. "Your Majesty, how may I be of service?"

"Indeed, sir," said Henry," something for me to do as well, I pray."

The King nodded. "Always by my side, John, and now I have

Henry as well."

"Indeed, sir," said Henry with a bow.

"Grayton, Lady Catherine has recently returned to London and has presented her plan on securing my cousins, Lady Sophie and Lady Juliet ..."

The Queen hemmed. "Indeed, such a plan. I fear it is already too late. We should have done something about the wretched woman days ago."

"Now Charlotte, we have discussed all the possibilities." He turned to Grayton. "John, I would wish it of you to accompany my Guards in escorting Catherine to the shores of France."

He bowed deeply. "Indeed, Your Majesty, I would be honoured."

Henry's chest swelled, his face stern, his shoulders held back. "Sir, I wish to be of service and go along."

"Indeed not, I need you here, Henry."

Just then the Queen's lady-in-waiting entered. "Beg pardon, ma'am, but you wanted to be informed immediately of their arrival. They are in your receiving room."

The Queen smiled. "Very well." She nodded and winked at His Majesty. Taking Grayton's hand, she smiled. "Good luck, John, God's speed." She gestured to Margaret and Henry. "Come along with me."

* * *

Lord Grayton rode pell-mell with the King's Captain of the Guards to a waiting ship. Already situated on deck sat Lady Catherine—well, now simply Catherine, stripped of her title and English return rights, she was banished forever.

But that didn't seem to trouble her, for she sat smug, a king's ransom tied securely to her waist.

Grayton gaped at the rope tied so securely about her person. "Do you think for an instant anyone on the King's vessel would dare grab your bag of gold, Catherine?"

The afternoon sea mist made her thick black hair frizzy about her sagging silk bonnet. Sniffing the air, she smirked. "One cannot be too careful, my lord."

"How prophetic you are, Catherine." He chuckled. "Well, where you're going you will need to be very careful."

"France?" she scoffed, "I'll buy my way like I have always done." She patted the heavy bag of gold at her waist and smirked.

"I shall have my way."

The wind picked up, and the ship began to roll, whistles blew, sailors scampered up the mast, the sails billowed full, the English flag flapping."

"Why," said Grayton looking up at the flag, "I do believe it is waving at you Catherine," he held a stern, placid face, "waving goodbye, that is."

She shook her head with a sigh. "You have always been a simpleton, Grayton." Glancing up at the flag, she smirked. "It flaps in the breeze very much like Sophie and Juliet are now flapping about, dangling perhaps," she snickered.

His face turned red. "What do you mean?"

She smirked. "Well, once delivered onto French soil you shall see."

Just at that moment, the Captain's whistle blew. "Guards, be alert!" He stood on the main deck squinting through his brass spyglass. "A vessel approaches from the Continent."

The late afternoon sun had broken through. The choppy waves were foamy white, the wind picked up. The white cliffs of Dover now out of sight.

"Steady as she goes," commanded the Captain in such a tone.

That little brown speck of a boat that was approaching was now much larger, very much larger.

Catherine squinted out at the object. "Why, it is not a boat at all, but a ..."

"Battleship!" The Captain shouted, "All hands on deck!" His ruddy cheeks red and full as he blew his whistle. "I don't believe my eyes. Why, it's the *Fantasque*, French Admiral Suffren's ship. What is he doing in these waters?"

The magnificent French ship was now within shouting distance. French sailors shouted: "Honneur, Patrie, Valeur, Discipline!" The French Admiral stood looking stern, his one hand tucked neatly into his vest pocket. "Preparer a mourir!"

Catherine gasped, clasping the ransom gold her breast. "Oh, this is not the plan at all! I was to be set on French soil, alone ..."

Steadying himself, Grayton seised the ship's rail. "Look at the size of that canon, the Admiral has it aimed directly at your head, Catherine." He backed up. "Oh, dare I bear witness to such terror?"

She jumped up and ran toward the bow of the ship screaming hysterically, waving her arms at the French Admiral. "Here, here, it is gold. It is all yours, rescue me! Oh, rescue me from these English dogs."

"Madam," said the captain grabbing her hand, "they will gladly take the gold and kill you. If you want our protection, you must at once tell us where you have hidden Lady Sophie and Lady Juliet."

She pulled away from his hold and ran to the rail. Climbing up, she waved frantically to the French sailors, "I have gold, see for yourselves!" She clasped the bag. "Rescue me, it is yours ..."

Laughing, the *French Admiral* smirked. "Toss me a few coins, and we shall see, mademoiselle."

As she frantically grappled inside the bag, she brought out a ... stone? Looking at the rubble, she stared in disbelief, "Why, this is not gold." As she tried to untie her booty, Grayton reached for her. Sneering, she kicked him in the face. "You killed my sister, I hope you die."

Grayton fell back onto the deck, holding his face, blood ran through his fingers.

The captain ran to help his lordship, kneeling by his side, he shouted up at her, "Come down at once, madam. That is not a French ship, he is not an admiral! All along it has been a ruse ..."

"What?" with a look of horror, she glanced at the *French Admiral*. He and the *French* sailors were laughing. A sudden mighty gust of wind picked up, and she, weighted down with her ransom rubble, slipped.

Grayton tried to grab her, but she slid between both bows of the English vessels and just before disappearing into the choppy, greenish-black waters, screamed, "They are dead!"

* * *

Hurrying back to the palace, Grayton was inconsolable. "I shall never find them now. My beautiful Jane is really gone." Keeping his head in his hands, he could not look out at the beautiful English countryside without weeping. "I shall never set foot in Rosewood Park again, I shall never visit Holybourne, I shall never again see Alton." Burying his head in his hands, he wept, "I want no more of this life."

When his lordship's carriage entered St. James Palace, his tears had evaporated. His eyes were now rimmed pink, hollow and ringed black. Blood still caked about his lips, his nose was swollen and painful. His hair wind-blown, black stubble grew harsh about his face and neck.

"Father?"

Grayton's carriage had stopped beneath the carriage-porch at the palace. He remained sitting, staring blankly. He waved off the royal servant who stood obediently holding the open carriage door. It had begun to rain. "What?" he muttered at a noise someone had uttered.

Margaret climbed into his carriage and took up his hand. "Dear God, Father, what has happened to you?"

His lordship slowly turned his head and looked into her tearful eyes. "Margaret?"

"Yes, Papa?"

"Why are you crying, Margaret?"

"You have been sitting here for well over an hour ... staring at nothing, Papa."

He pressed her hand. "Your Aunt Catherine is dead, Margaret."

"We know, Papa."

"She said I killed your mother, Margaret."

"Sir, you did nothing of the sort. You only killed the ugly, greedy, nasty sort that dwells within each of us. But thanks to you, we are now a wholesome family, free from the shackles of preposterous notions of old."

Kissing her forehead, he shrugged. "Thank you, thank you."

"I must tell you the truth about ... about Jane and Anne, Papa."

He held up his hand. "No, I do not want to hear of it, Margaret. Please spare me." He wiped his eyes. "I cannot bear to hear the gruesome details."

Margaret looked at him incredulously. "But Papa, you do not understand."

"Daughter, please, let me keep her memory as I last saw her. I cannot hear another word of it."

She took his hand. "Very well, Papa, let us go in then and see His Majesty, he has been waiting for you."

With a deep sigh, he nodded. "Let us be done with it. I want nothing more than to return home."

As Margaret helped him from the carriage, he stumbled but caught himself. "No worries, I am but a little weary."

When they entered the palace even the low light from the candles made him squint in pain. "I suppose I look a little dishevelled, not worthy to face my King."

"He is anxious to see you, Papa. Everyone is."

"Everyone?"

"Mary, Victoria, Lizzy, Henry ..."

"Indeed, all I have left in life." Putting his arms her, he hugged her. "Indeed, how loyal all of you have remained, loving and forgiving." Tears slid down his bloodied face.

As they approached the King's chamber, the guards opened the door.

Slowly entering the room, Grayton lifted his head and found Jane hurrying to his side. "Jane?" He rubbed his swollen eyes and winced, "Jane?"

"God in heaven, John, what has happened to you?" She gently took up his bloodied hand and held it to her lips.

"Bring my physician, make haste," shouted the King. "Good God, Grayton. I heard you were in a scuffle ... but they did not tell me you were beaten. Come, my good man and sit."

Jane steadied him to the sofa. "Henry, the Whitmores and Granny are all safe. They are in the next room."

Looking astonished, his jaw dropped. "They are unharmed? Catherine said you were all dead."

"Oh, my lordship, we were all sworn to secrecy."

"We have known about Catherine for quite a while, John," said the Queen.

"We dared not tell you or Henry of our plans. There was a spy ..."

"We have been in the palace all this time," said Jane.

"Even during His Majesty's ball?" said Grayton.

She nodded. "We were told not to say a word ... there was a spy somewhere in the palace, and we were sworn to secrecy. We most recently learned we were to be stolen and killed."

"I could not allow another soul to know, Grayton," said the King apologetically. "When I sent you to escort Lady Catherine to France, I had no idea she was so ruthless. Mrs Helen Whitmore was their Governess, and it was she who came to us months ago fearful something dreadful was in the offing. We devised a ploy, thinking Catherine would confess her greed, plead for mercy once looking into the barrel of a ship's cannon. I never thought she would give up England so easily."

"Indeed, a bag of gold is a mighty anchor, sir."

When the King's physician rushed into the room, Jane stood. "Here, sir." She gently let go his hand. "Sir, you must now rest." She turned to leave.

Grayton stood. "No, Jane, I'll not rest ..." Wincing in pain, he knelt and took her hand. "Jane, my beloved, will you marry me?"